"A magnificent novel, tonally flawless, its humor defiant in the face of vast tragedy."
 — Joan London,
author of *Gilgamesh* and *The Good Parents*

"The impossibly moving story of two damaged youths who forge from their amour fou a love that will light the decades ahead. With playfulness and charm, with iron conviction, *Fever at Dawn* will convince you that it's possible not only to survive the worst of human hell, but to transcend it."
 — Francisco Goldman, author of *Say Her Name*

"*Fever at Dawn* belongs to the canon of extraordinary true stories about love and war and the power of letters. Dramatic, compassionate and deeply moving, this unforgettable story reminds us that the Holocaust is not only history, it's a warning."
 — Jennifer Clement, author of *Prayers for the Stolen*

"A riveting and high-spirited journey from the brink of death toward life, a novel that asserts the power of love in a world newly devastated by unspeakable hate. With courage, humor, and unfailing emotional honesty, Péter Gárdos illuminates the incredible power of the human will — the drive not just to stay alive, but to fight for a life worth celebrating."
 — Julie Orringer, author of *The Invisible Bridge*

"Will make you like life more when you've finished." — *Bookseller*

FEVER AT DAWN

Péter Gárdos

Translated from the Hungarian by Elizabeth Szász

Mariner Books
Houghton Mifflin Harcourt
Boston   New York

First Mariner Books edition 2017
Copyright © 2015 by Péter Gárdos
English translation © 2016 by Elizabeth Szász
Reading Group Guide copyright © 2017 by Houghton Mifflin Harcourt
Publishing Company

Published by arrangement with Libri Kiadó.
First published in English by The Text Publishing Company, Australia 2016.

For information about permission to reproduce selections from this book, write to
trade.permissions@hmhco.com or to Permissions, Houghton Mifflin Harcourt
Publishing Company, 3 Park Avenue, 19th Floor, New York, New York 10016.

www.hmhco.com

Library of Congress Cataloging-in-Publication Data
Names: Gárdos, Péter, date, author. | Szász, Elizabeth.
Title: Fever at dawn / Péter Gárdos ; translated from the Hungarian by Elizabeth Szász.
Other titles: Hajnali láz. English
Description: First U.S. edition. | Boston : Houghton Mifflin Harcourt, 2016. |
Description based on print version record and CIP data provided by publisher;
resource not viewed.
Identifiers: LCCN 2016004111 (print) | LCCN 2015046794 (ebook) |
ISBN 978–0-544-77033-1 (ebook) | ISBN 978-0-544-76979-3 (hardcover) |
ISBN 978-0-544-94441-1 (pbk.)
Classification: LCC PH3382.17.A37 (print) | LCC PH3382.17.A37 H3513 2016 (ebook) |
DDC 894/.51134 — dc23
LC record available at http://lccn.loc.gov/2016004111

Printed in the United States of America
DOC 10 9 8 7 6 5 4 3 2 1

FEVER AT DAWN

One

MY FATHER, Miklós, sailed to Sweden on a rainy summer's day three weeks after the Second World War ended. He was twenty-five years old. An angry north wind lashed the Baltic Sea into a three-metre swell, and he lay on the lower deck while the ship plunged and bucked. Around him, passengers clung desperately to their straw mattresses.

They had been at sea for less than an hour when Miklós was taken ill. He began to cough up bloody foam, and then he started to wheeze so loudly that he almost drowned out the waves pounding the hull. He was one of the more serious cases, parked in the first row right next to the swing door. Two sailors picked up his skeletal body and carried him into a nearby cabin.

The doctor didn't hesitate. There was no time for pain-killers. Relying on luck to hit the right spot between two ribs, he stuck a large needle into my father's chest. Half a litre of fluid drained from his lungs. When the aspirator arrived, the doctor swapped the needle for a plastic tube and siphoned off another litre and a half of mucus.

Miklós felt better.

When the captain learned that the doctor had saved a passenger's life, he granted the sick man a special favour: he had him wrapped in a thick blanket and taken out to sit on the deck. Heavy clouds were gathering over the granite water. The captain, impeccable in his uniform, stood beside Miklós's deckchair.

'Do you speak German?' he asked.

'Yes.'

'Congratulations on your survival.'

In different circumstances, this conversation might have led somewhere. But Miklós was in no state to chat. It was all he could do to acknowledge the situation.

'I'm alive.'

The captain looked him up and down. My father's ashen skin was stretched over his skull, and there were ugly warts on his face. His pupils were magnified by his glasses, and his mouth was a dark yawning void. He virtually hadn't a tooth to call his own. I'm not quite sure why. Maybe three burly louts had beaten his scrawny frame to a pulp in an air-raid shelter lit by a naked bulb swinging from the ceiling. Maybe one of these thugs had grabbed a flat iron and used it over and over to bash Miklós in the face. According to the official version, which was rather short on detail, most of his teeth had been knocked out in the prison on Margit Street in Budapest in 1944, when he was arrested as a deserter from a Jewish forced-labour unit.

But now he was alive. And despite the slight whistle when he took a breath his lungs were dutifully processing the crisp salty air.

The captain peered through his telescope. 'We're docking in Malmö for five minutes.'

This didn't really mean anything to Miklós. He was one of 224 concentration-camp survivors who were being shipped from Lübeck in Germany to Stockholm. Some of them were in such bad shape that they wanted nothing more than to survive the journey. A few minutes in Malmö was neither here nor there.

The captain, however, continued to explain the decision, as if to a superior. 'The order came over the radio. This stop wasn't part of my itinerary.'

The ship's horn sounded as the docks of Malmö harbour became visible in the mist. A flock of seagulls circled.

The ship moored at the end of the pier. Two sailors disembarked and started jogging along the pier. Between them they carried a big empty basket—the kind washerwomen use to haul wet laundry up to the attic to hang out.

A crowd of women on bicycles was waiting at the approach to the pier. There must have been fifty of them, motionless and silent, gripping their handlebars. Many wore black headscarves.

They looked like ravens perched on a branch. It was only when the sailors reached the barrier that Miklós noticed the parcels and baskets hanging from the handlebars.

He felt the captain's hand on his shoulder. 'Some mad rabbi by the name of Kronheim dreamed this up,' the captain explained. 'He placed an ad in the papers saying that you people were arriving on this ship. He even managed to arrange for us to dock here.'

Each of the women dropped her parcel into the big laundry basket. One standing slightly back let go of her handlebars and her bicycle fell over. From where he sat on deck, Miklós heard the clang of the metal on the cobblestones. Given the length of the pier, this is quite inconceivable, yet whenever my father told this story he always included the clang.

Once they had collected all the packages, the sailors jogged back to the ship. This scene remained fixed in Miklós's mind: an improbably empty pier, the sailors running with the basket, and in the background the strange motionless army of women and their bicycles.

The parcels contained biscuits that these nameless women had baked to celebrate the arrival of the survivors in Sweden. As my father tasted the soft, buttery pastry in his toothless mouth, he could detect vanilla and raspberry, flavours so unfamiliar after years of camp food that he almost had to relearn them.

'Sweden welcomes you,' grunted the captain, as he turned away to give orders. The ship was already heading out to sea.

Miklós sat savouring his biscuits. High among the clouds, a

biplane drew away, dipping its wings in salute. When he saw it, my father began to feel he was truly alive.

~

By the end of the first week in July 1945, Miklós was in a crowded sixteen-bed hospital ward, a barracks-like wooden hut in a remote village called Lärbro on the island of Gotland. Propped up against a pillow, he was writing a letter. Sunlight poured through the window and nurses in crisply starched blouses, white bonnets and long linen skirts darted between the beds.

He had beautiful handwriting: shapely letters, elegant loops and just a hair's breadth between each word. When he finished his letter he put it in an envelope, sealed it and leaned it against the jug of water on his bedside table. Two hours later a nurse called Katrin picked it up and dropped it in the postbox with the other patients' mail.

Miklós rarely got out of his hospital bed, but two weeks after writing his letter he was allowed to sit out in the corridor. Each morning the post was handed out, and one day a letter came for him—straight from the Swedish Office for Refugees. It contained the names and addresses of 117 women, all of them young Hungarians whom nurses and doctors were trying to bring back to life in various temporary hospitals across Sweden. Miklós transcribed their details into a thin exercise book with square-ruled paper he had found somewhere.

By this time he had recovered from the dramatic pronouncement he had received a few days earlier.

~

Pressed against the X-ray machine, Miklós had done his best not to move. Dr Lindholm shouted at him from the other room. The doctor was a gangling figure, at least six foot six tall, and he spoke a funny sort of Hungarian. All his long vowels sounded the same, as if he were blowing up a balloon. He had run the Lärbro hospital—now temporarily enlarged to accommodate the intake of camp survivors—for the last dozen years. His wife, Márta, a tiny woman whom Miklós reckoned couldn't be more than four foot six, was a nurse and worked in the hospital too; she was Hungarian, which explained why the doctor tackled the language with such bravado.

'You hold breath! No frisking!' he bellowed.

A click and a hum—the X-ray was ready. Miklós relaxed his shoulders.

Dr Lindholm walked over and stood beside him, gazing with compassion at a point slightly above his head. Miklós was slumped, his sunken chest naked against the machine, as if he never wanted to get dressed again. His glasses had steamed up.

'What you say you occupied with, Miklós?' the doctor asked.

'I was a journalist. And poet.'

'Ah! Engineer of the soul. Very good.'

Miklós shifted from one foot to the other. He was cold.

'Dress. Why you stand around?'

Miklós shuffled over to the corner of the room and pulled on his pyjama jacket. 'Is there a problem?' he asked the doctor.

Lindholm still didn't look at him. He started walking towards his office, waving at Miklós to follow him. He was muttering, almost to himself, 'Is a problem.'

Erik Lindholm's office looked onto the garden. On these warm midsummer evenings the island glittered in a bronze light that bathed the countryside. The dark furniture radiated comfort and safety.

Miklós sat in a leather armchair. Opposite him, on the other side of the desk, sat Dr Lindholm. He had changed into a smart waistcoat. He was flicking anxiously through Miklós's medical reports. He switched on the sea-green glass desk lamp, though there was no real need for it.

'How much you weigh now, Miklós?'

'Forty-seven kilos.'

'You see. It works like a clock.'

As a result of Dr Lindholm's strict diet, Miklós had gained eighteen kilos in only a few weeks. My father kept buttoning and unbuttoning his pyjama jacket, which was far too big for him.

'What temperature you have this morning?'

'Thirty-eight point two.'

Dr Lindholm put the reports down on his desk. 'I won't beat away the bush any longer. Is that what they say? You are quite strong now to face facts.'

Miklós smiled. Almost all his teeth were made of a palladiumbased metal alloy that was acid-resistant, cheap and ugly. The day after he'd arrived in Lärbro, a dentist had come to see him. He took moulds of his mouth and warned him that the temporary plate he was getting would be more practical than aesthetic. In a trice the dentist had fitted the metal into his mouth.

Although Miklós's smile was anything but heart-warming, Dr Lindholm forced himself to look directly at him.

'I come straight at the point,' he said. 'It is easier. Six months. You have six months to live, Miklós.' He picked up an X-ray and held it to the light. 'Look. Come closer.'

Miklós obligingly stood up and hunched over the desk. Dr Lindholm's slender fingers roamed over the contoured landscape of the X-ray.

'Here, here, here and here. You see, Miklós? See these patches? This is your tuberculosis. Permanent damage. Nothing to be done about them, I'm afraid. Terrible thing, I have to say. In everyday words, the illness … gobbles the lungs. Can one say "gobble" in Hungarian?'

They stared at the X-ray. Miklós held himself up against the desk. He wasn't feeling very strong, but he managed a nod, thus confirming that the doctor had found a way through the tangle of his language. 'Gobble' was accurate enough to show what the future had in store for him; he didn't need technical terminology. After all, his father had owned a bookshop in Debrecen before the war. It was housed in Gambrinus Court in the Bishop's Palace, under the arcades, a few minutes' walk from the main square. The shop was named Gambrinus Booksellers and consisted of three narrow, high-ceilinged rooms. In one room you could also buy stationery, and there was a lending library too. As a teenager Miklós would perch on top of the high wooden ladder and read books from all over the world—so he could certainly appreciate Lindholm's poetic turn of phrase.

Dr Lindholm continued to stare into my father's eyes. 'As matters stand,' he explained, 'medical science says that you are too gone to come back. There will be good days. And bad ones. I will always be next to you. But I don't want to lead you up the path. You have six months. Seven at most. My heart is heavy, but that is the truth.'

Miklós straightened up, smiling, and then flopped back into the roomy armchair. He seemed almost cheerful. The doctor wasn't quite sure that he had understood or even heard the diagnosis. But Miklós was thinking of things far more important than his health.

Two

TWO DAYS after this conversation Miklós was allowed out for short walks in the beautiful hospital garden. He sat on one of the benches in the shade of a big tree with spreading branches. He rarely looked up. He wrote letter after letter, in pencil, in that attractive looping hand of his, using the hardcover Swedish edition of a novel by Martin Andersen Nexø as a desk. Miklós admired Nexø's political views and the silent courage of the workers in his books. Perhaps he remembered that the famous Danish author had also suffered from tuberculosis. Miklós wrote swiftly, placing a stone on the finished letters to stop the wind blowing them away.

The next day he knocked on Dr Lindholm's door. He was determined to charm the good doctor with his frankness. He needed his help.

At this time of day it was Dr Lindholm's custom to talk to his patients while seated on his sofa. He sat at one end in his white coat, while Miklós sat at the other end in his pyjamas.

The doctor fingered the stack of envelopes with surprise. 'Is not in tradition to ask patients who they write to and why. And not curiosity now that … ' he mumbled.

'I know,' said Miklós. 'But I definitely want to let you in on this.'

'And there are 117 envelopes here? I congratulate you for diligence.' Dr Lindholm raised his arm as if he were gauging the weight of the letters. 'I ask the nurse to buy stamps for them,' he said obligingly. 'Always feel free to apply me for help in any financial matter.'

Miklós nonchalantly crossed his pyjama-clad legs, and grinned. 'All women.'

Dr Lindholm raised an eyebrow. 'Is that so?'

'Or rather, young women,' my father corrected. 'Hungarian girls. From the Debrecen region. That's where I was born.'

'I see,' said the doctor.

But he didn't. He hadn't a clue what Miklós intended with that pile of letters. He gave my father a sympathetic look—after all, this was a man who had been sentenced to death.

'A few weeks ago,' Miklós went on eagerly, 'I made an enquiry about women survivors convalescing in Sweden who were born in or near Debrecen. Only those under thirty!'

'In hospitals? My God!'

They both knew that in addition to Lärbro there were a number of rehabilitation centres operating in Sweden. Miklós sat up straight. He was proud of his strategy. 'And there are loads of girls in them,' he went on excitedly. 'Here's the list of names.'

He took the sheet of paper out of his pocket and, blushing, handed it to Dr Lindholm. The names had been carefully assessed. He'd put a cross, a tick or a small triangle beside each one.

'Aha! You look for acquaintances,' exclaimed Dr Lindholm. 'I'm in favour of that.'

'You're mistaken,' said Miklós with a wink and a smile. 'I'm looking for a wife. I'd like to get married!'

At last it was out.

Dr Lindholm frowned. 'It seems, my dear Miklós, that I did not speak myself clearly the other day.'

'You did, you did,' Miklós reassured him.

'The language is against me! Six months. Is all you have left. You know, when a doctor must say something like this, is dreadful.'

'I understood you perfectly, Dr Lindholm,' said Miklós.

They sat in uncomfortable silence, each on his end of the sofa. Dr Lindholm was trying to work out whether he should lecture someone who had been sentenced to death. Was it his job to beg his patient to think sensibly? Miklós was wondering whether it was worth trying to persuade Dr Lindholm, with all his experience, to look on the bright side of things. The upshot was they left each other in peace.

That afternoon Miklós got into bed as prescribed and lay back on his pillows. It was four o'clock—nap time. Some of the patients in his hut were asleep, and others were playing cards. His friend Harry was practising the trickiest part of the last movement of a romantic sonata on his violin, over and over, with aggravating zeal.

Miklós was sticking stamps on his 117 envelopes. He licked and stuck, licked and stuck. When his mouth became dry he took a sip from the glass of water on his bedside table. He must have felt that Harry's violin was an appropriate accompaniment to this activity. The 117 letters could have been written with carbon paper. They were identical except for one thing—the name of the addressee.

~

Did Miklós ever wonder what these girls might feel when they opened the envelopes addressed to them? What did they think when they took out the letters and began to read his neat, swirling handwriting?

Oh, those girls! Sitting on the edges of their beds, on garden benches, in the corners of disinfected corridors, in front of thickened glass windows, stopping for a moment on worn staircases, under spreading lime trees, on the banks of miniature lakes, leaning against cold yellow tiles. Did my father see them in his mind's eye as they unfolded the letters in their nightdresses or in the pale grey uniforms they wore in the rehabilitation centres? Confused at first, later smiling perhaps, heartbeat accelerating, skimming the lines over and over in astonishment.

> Dear Nora, Dear Erzsébet, Dear Lili, Dear Zsuzsa, Dear Sára, Dear Seréna, Dear Ágnes, Dear Giza, Dear Baba, Dear Katalin, Dear Judit, Dear Gabriella …
>
> You are probably used to strangers chatting you up when you speak Hungarian, for no better reason than they are Hungarian too. We men can be so bad-mannered. For example, I addressed you by your first name on the pretext that we grew up in the same town. I don't know whether you already know me from Debrecen. Until my homeland ordered me to 'volunteer' for forced labour, I worked for the *Independent* newspaper, and my father owned a bookshop in Gambrinus Court.
>
> Judging by your name and age, I have a feeling that I might know you. Did you by any chance ever live in Gambrinus Court?
>
> Excuse me for writing in pencil, but I'm confined to bed for a few days on doctor's orders, and we're not allowed to use ink in bed.

~

Lili Reich was one of the 117 women who received a letter. She was an eighteen-year-old patient at the Smålandsstenar rehabilitation hospital. It was early September. She opened the envelope and scanned its contents. The young man from distant Lärbro did have lovely handwriting. But he must have mixed her up with someone else. She promptly forgot the whole thing.

Besides, she was terribly excited about her own plans. A few days earlier she and her two new girlfriends, Sára Stern and Judit Gold, had decided to put an end to the grey days of slow recuperation and set their hearts on staging an evening of Hungarian music in the hospital hall.

Lili had studied piano for eight years, Sára had sung in a choir and Judit had taken dance lessons. Judit had a large, pale face with fine dark hairs above her thin, rather severe lips. Quite the opposite of Sára, who was blonde and light boned with narrow shoulders and shapely legs. Two other girls, Erika Friedmann and Gitta Pláner, joined in just for fun. They banged out three copies of the thirty-minute program on the typewriter in the doctors' room and pinned them up around the hospital. On the night of the performance, the creaky wooden chairs in the hall filled with patients and curious visitors from the nearby village of Smålandsstenar.

The concert was a resounding success. After the last piece, a lively Hungarian dance, the *csárdás*, the audience gave the five blushing girls a standing ovation.

As she ran offstage, Lili felt a sudden unbearable pain in

her stomach. She hunched over, pressing her hand to her belly, moaning. And then she lay down; her forehead was bathed in sweat.

'What's the matter, Lili?' asked Sára, who had become her closest friend, crouching down beside her.

'It hurts dreadfully,' she said, and passed out.

Lili couldn't remember being put in the ambulance. She could only recall Sára's blurry face saying something she couldn't hear.

Later, she would often think that without this pain, which had something to do with her kidneys, she might never have met Miklós. If that hulking white ambulance hadn't taken her to the military hospital more than a hundred kilometres away in Eksjö; if, when she came to visit, Judit hadn't brought Miklós's letter, along with her toothbrush and diary; if, on that visit, Judit hadn't persuaded her, against all common sense, to write a few words to the nice young man (for the sake of humanity if nothing else); that's where the story would have ended.

But as it happened, on one of those interminable hospital evenings, once the noise filtering in from the corridor and the clanging of the old-fashioned lift with its grating doors had ebbed away and the bulb above her bed was casting a pale light onto her blanket, Lili took a sheet of paper and, after a bit of thought, started to write.

Dear Miklós,
I'm unlikely to be the person you were thinking

of, because, though I was born in Debrecen, I lived
in Budapest from the age of one. Nonetheless, I've
thought a lot about you. Your friendly letter was so
comforting that I would be happy for you to write
again.

That was a half-truth, of course. Confined to bed with a
strange new illness, out of fear, by way of escape or just to stave
off boredom, Lili allowed herself to daydream.

As for myself, neatly ironed trousers or a smart haircut
don't do anything. What touches me is the value
inside someone.

~

Miklós had grown a little stronger. He could now walk into town
with Harry. Each of the patients received five kronor a week
pocket money. There were two cake shops in Lärbro. One of
them had small round marble tables just like a café in Hungary.
On the way there, Miklós and Harry ran into Kristin, a plump
Swedish hairdresser, and Harry urged her to join them. So now
the three of them were sitting at a marble table in a corner of
the cake shop. Kristin was politely eating apple pie with a fork.
The men each had a glass of soda water. They were speaking
German, because the Hungarians were only just getting used to
the melodic Swedish language.

'You are two very nice guys,' declared Kristin, the sugar

from the icing trembling on her pale moustache. 'Where were you born exactly?'

Miklós sat up. 'In Hajdúnánás,' he boasted, as if he had uttered a magic word.

'And I was born in Sajószentpéter,' said Harry.

Kristin naturally attempted the impossible—to repeat what she'd heard. It sounded as if she were gargling. 'Haydu ... nana ... Sayu ... sent ... peter ...'

They laughed. Kristin nibbled her apple pie. This gave Harry time to think up a joke. He was good at jokes.

'What did Adam say to Eve when they first met?' he asked.

So keen was Kristin to work out the answer that she forgot to chew. Harry waited a bit, then stood up, miming that he was now stark naked.

'Please, my lady, stand aside, because I'm not sure how much this thingamajig will grow!' he declared, pointing down towards his fly.

Kristin didn't understand at first, but then she blushed.

Miklós felt ashamed and took a sip of his soda. Harry, though, was just getting started.

'Here's another one,' he blurted. 'The lady of the house asked the new chambermaid if her references were good. The chambermaid nodded. "Yes, madam, they were satisfied with me everywhere." "Can you cook?" The chambermaid nodded. "Do you like children?" The chambermaid nodded. "Yes, I do, but it's better when the master of the house is careful."'

Kristin giggled. Harry grabbed her hand and kissed it fervently. Kristin was about to remove her hand, but Harry had a tight grip and she decided not to resist for a moment or two. Miklós took another sip of soda and looked away.

Then Kristin freed herself and got up, smoothing her skirt. 'I'm off to the ladies' room,' she announced, walking demurely across the café.

Harry switched to Hungarian right away. 'She only lives two blocks away.'

'How d'you know?'

'She said so. Don't you listen?'

'She likes you.'

'You, too.'

'For all I care,' replied Miklós, giving Harry a stern look.

'You haven't been in a café for years. You haven't seen a naked woman for years.'

'What's that got to do with it?' asked Miklós.

'At last we can get out of the hospital. We should start living!'

Kristin was now sashaying back to the table.

'What do you say to a sandwich?' whispered Harry, still in Hungarian.

'What sort of sandwich?'

'The two of us and her. Kristin in the middle.'

'Leave me out of it.'

Harry switched to German, almost in the same breath, and began to stroke Kristin's ankle under the table. 'I've been telling

Miklós that I've fallen head over heels for you, dear Kristin. Do I have any chance?'

Kristin put a warning finger coquettishly on Harry's mouth.

~

Kristin rented a tiny flat on the third floor of a building in Nysvägen Street. The low rumble of traffic filtered in through the open window. She sat on the bed so that Harry could get to her more easily. The first test she set him was to mend a tear in the strap of her bra. 'Are you finished yet?' she asked, monitoring the process in the mirror.

'Not quite. It'd be easier if you took it off.'

'I wouldn't dream of it.'

'You're torturing me.'

'That's the point. You should suffer. Restrain yourself. Do a bit of housework,' replied Kristin, giggling.

Harry finished at last, breaking the thread off with his teeth. Kristin went over to the mirror, turning around and fingering the mended strap.

Harry grew redder and redder. Then he hugged her and clumsily tried to undo the bra. 'I can cook, do the washing, scrub. I am a workhorse,' he whispered.

By way of an answer Kristin kissed him.

~

When Harry came back an hour later, he found Miklós at the same marble table in the corner of the café. He was writing a letter and didn't even look up when Harry flopped down beside him. The tip of his pencil seemed to glide over the white paper. Harry gave a deep dejected sigh.

When at last Miklós raised his head, he showed no surprise at Harry's dismal expression.

'Aren't you in love any more?'

Harry swigged the remains of the soda in Miklós's glass. 'In love? I'm a wreck.'

'What happened?'

'She made me mend her bra. Then I undressed her. Her skin was so silky and firm!'

'Good. Now don't interrupt me, I've got to finish this,' said Miklós, returning to his letter.

Harry envied the way that Miklós could cut himself off from everything with the merest flick of his finger. 'But *I* wasn't firm. It doesn't work,' he muttered. 'It simply doesn't work.'

Miklós kept writing. 'What doesn't work?'

'I don't. And I used to do it five times a day. I could walk up and down with a bucket of water hanging from it.'

'Hanging from what?' Miklós enquired, biting the end of his pencil.

'Right now ... a slug hangs between my legs. Soft, white and useless.'

Miklós found the right word. He smiled to himself and wrote it down, satisfied. Now he could comfort Harry.

'That's quite normal. Without feelings it doesn't work.'

Harry was chewing the side of his mouth in irritation. He slid the letter across the table and started to read. '"Dear Lili, I am twenty-five—"'

Miklós snatched at the letter. There was a brief tug of war, which Miklós won. He thrust the letter into his pocket.

> Dear Lili,
>
> I am twenty-five. I used to be a journalist until the First Jewish Law got me thrown out of my job.

Miklós had a special gift for poetic licence. The truth was that he had been a journalist for exactly eight and a half days. He was taken on at the Debrecen *Independent* on a Monday, more as messenger boy on the police rounds than an actual journalist. It was the worst possible moment. The following week a law banning Jews from certain professions came into force. His newspaper career was over. But he kept that brief apprenticeship on his CV for the rest of his life. It can't have been easy for a nineteen-year-old to get over such a setback. One day he had a pencil behind his ear; the next he was shouting, 'Soda! Come and get your soda water!' as he leaned out from a horse-drawn cart and a bitter wind whistled around his ears.

> After that I worked in a textile factory, then as a
> bloodhound in a credit agency; I had a job as a clerk,
> an advertising salesman and other similar excellent
> posts until 1941, when I was called up for forced
> labour. At the first opportunity, I escaped to the

Russians. I spent a month washing dishes in a big restaurant in Csernovic before I joined a partisan group in Bukovina.

There were eight Hungarian deserters. The Red Army gave them a crash course in spying and dropped them behind German lines. Looking back, it's obvious that the Russians didn't trust them. The lessons of history teach us that the Soviets didn't trust anybody. But when those Hungarian deserters turned up, they decided to enlist them.

I can imagine my father wearing a quilted jacket and a knapsack, clinging to the open door of an aeroplane. He looks down. Below him there's vertical space, clouds, and spreading countryside. He suffers from vertigo, feels dizzy, turns away and starts to vomit. Rough hands grab him from behind and shove him into the void.

On that dawn morning, somewhere in the vicinity of Nagyvárad, Hungarian soldiers with submachine guns were waiting in open woodland. When the parachute team floated just a few metres above the ground, the soldiers casually fired off a few rounds for target practice. Miklós was lucky. He was the only one they didn't hit. But as soon as he landed, they pounced on him and put him in handcuffs. That night he was transported to a prison in Budapest where, in the space of barely half an hour, he was relieved of most of his teeth.

~

In the café in Lärbro, Harry looked at Miklós with admiration. 'How many have replied?'

'Eighteen.'

'Are you going to write back to all of them?'

'Some of them, but she's the one,' Miklós answered, patting the pocket where he had hidden the letter.

> I've introduced myself, now it's your turn, Lili. First of all, please send a photo! Then tell me everything about yourself.

'How do you know?'

'I just do.'

Three

LILI BLEW her nose and wiped away her tears. It was the end of September. She was in a four-bed ward on the third floor of the Eksjö hospital. Outside the window stood a lonely birch tree that had already shed its leaves for winter.

Dr Svensson had started going bald early. He wasn't yet forty, but pink skin, reminiscent of a baby's bottom, was already shining through his colourless hair. He was short and stocky, and his hands were like a child's. His thumbnails were the size of cherry-blossom petals.

He removed his protective apron of leather and wire mesh, and wandered into the bleak X-ray room. Beside the ugly apparatus there was a single chair on which Lili was sitting. She looked pale and scared in her washed-out striped hospital overall.

Dr Svensson squatted down beside her and touched her hand. It was encouraging that the Hungarian girl spoke excellent German. Nuances counted a lot in this context.

'I've assessed your last X-ray. This new one will be ready tomorrow. We suspected scarlet fever at first, but we've excluded that now.'

'Something worse?' whispered Lili, as if they were in the audience at the theatre.

'Worse in some ways. It's not an infection. But there's no need to worry.'

'What's the matter with me?'

'That kidney of yours is behaving badly. But I'll cure you, I promise.'

Lili started to cry.

Dr Svensson took her hand. 'Please don't cry! You'll have to stay in bed again. This time we'll have to be stricter.'

'How long?'

'Two weeks to start with. Or three. Then we'll see,' he said, taking out his handkerchief.

> I haven't got a photo of myself. I've been back in
> hospital again for the past few days.

~

I hate dancing, but I love having fun—and eating stuffed peppers (in thick tomato sauce, of course).

The story goes that Miklós wasn't even nine years old when, with his hair dampened down and wearing a suit that felt like armour, he was dragged along to a dance at the Golden Bull Hotel. He was already having trouble with his eyes, and due to some sort of refraction error he had to wear glasses with thick, ugly lenses that did nothing for his looks.

At an energetic moment in the dance, the young Miklós and a little girl named Melinda were shoved into the middle of a circle of girls. The crowd of dancers clapped wildly and urged the pair to start spinning. Melinda came to life. Swept up by the wave of good cheer, she grabbed Miklós's hands and swirled round with him, until he slipped on the waxed parquet floor. And from this ignominious position he watched Melinda become the belle of the ball.

Now Miklós and Harry hurried back to the hospital. A strong wind was blowing. Miklós turned up the collar of his thin spring coat.

Harry stopped and took Miklós's arm. 'Ask her if she's got a girlfriend.'

'Not so fast. We're only at the beginning.'

That day the men had a party. They turned the barracks upside down, pushing the beds into the corners. They borrowed a guitar from somewhere, and it turned out that Jenö Grieger could at least strum the latest hits.

The dancing began. At first they just threw themselves around with abandon, then the urge to play different characters took over. They didn't discuss parts or assign roles, but began to act out dashing hussars and flirtatious girls. They clicked their heels. They curtsied; they whispered sweet nothings. They fawned over each other, swirling and spinning. Instincts that had been buried for months erupted.

Miklós didn't take part in this childish game. In silent lonely protest, he settled himself on his barricaded bed. He leaned his back against the wall, put his favourite book by Nexø across his knees, and began to write.

> You didn't say anything about your appearance!
> Now you're probably thinking that I'm some shallow
> Budapest type who only cares about that sort of thing.
> I'll let you in on a secret: I'm not.

~

Someone was knocking. Lili didn't even look up. She was reading a dog-eared German edition of *Dick Sand: A Captain at Fifteen* by Jules Verne, which Dr Svensson had given her the day before.

Sára Stern was standing in the doorway. Lili stared in shock. Sára rushed over to the bed, kneeled down and gave her a hug. The novel slipped to the floor.

'Dr Svensson gave me a referral. Right here, to this ward. Though there's nothing wrong with me.' Sára swirled round like a ballroom dancer. She undressed quickly, pulled on her night-dress and got into the bed next to Lili's.

Lili laughed and laughed as if she'd gone mad.

> Now I'll try to describe myself, since I don't have a photo. As far as my figure goes, I'd say I was plumpish (thanks to the Swedes), medium tall, with dark brown hair. My eyes are greyish-blue, my lips are thin, and my complexion is dark. You can imagine me as pretty or ugly, as you like. For my part, I make no comment. I have a picture of you in my mind. I wonder how close to reality it is.

~

On Sunday Dr Lindholm organised three buses to take his patients to the Gotland coast twenty kilometres away. Miklós and Harry wandered off from the others and found a deserted, sandy bay where they could be on their own. The radiant afternoon was a gift from heaven. The sky was like a stretched cobalt canvas. They took their shoes off and paddled in the shallows.

Later, Harry, who had taken to putting his virility to the test at every opportunity, disappeared behind a rock. Miklós pretended not to notice. The late afternoon cast long shadows. The silhouette of the invisible man, doggedly trying to satisfy himself, was projected onto the sand like a drawing by Egon Schiele. Miklós, meanwhile, tried to concentrate on the waves and the endless blue horizon.

I'd be interested to know what your views are about socialism. I gather from what you write about your family that you are middle class, just as I was until I became acquainted with Marxism—which the middle class tend to have very strange notions about.

~

Autumn came early in Eksjö. It came at night with unexpected swiftness, bringing with it sleet and a howling wind. The two girls watched in alarm as the lone birch tree swayed in the storm. The two beds were close enough for them to hold hands.

'If only I had twelve kronor!' whispered Lili.

'What would you do with it?'

Lili closed her eyes. 'There used to be a greengrocer on the corner of Nefelejts Street. My mother always sent me there to buy fruit.'

'I know the one. He was called Mr Teddy!'

'I don't remember that.'

'I do. His name was Mr Teddy. Though I called him Bear. What made you think of him?'

'Nothing really. Last month, before I got sick, I saw a dish of green peppers in a shop window in Smålandsstenar.'

'Really? I didn't think they had green peppers here.'

'Nor did I. They were twelve kronor—for a kilo, I suppose. Or was it half a kilo?'

'You had a craving for one?'

'I know it's silly, but I dreamed about those peppers yesterday. I bit into one. It was crisp. Fancy dreaming such a crazy thing.'

The sleet kept beating against the window. The two girls looked on wistfully.

> My friend Sára has been telling me a lot about
> socialism. I must admit I haven't taken much notice
> of politics so far. I'm reading a book about the show
> trials in Moscow in the 1930s. You probably know all
> about them.

~

A week or two later, in the middle of October, Miklós again felt he was going to suffocate. He didn't have time to shout out. He stood in the middle of the barracks, his body rigid, his mouth open, trying to suck in some oxygen. Then he collapsed.

This time they drained two litres of fluid from his lungs. He spent the rest of the night in a tiny room beside the surgery. Harry lay on the cold pinewood floor beside the bed so that he could let Dr Lindholm know right away if Miklós suffered another attack—though the doctor had tried to reassure him that another emergency was unlikely for a while now.

'What happened?' My father's voice fluttered in the air like a bird with a hurt wing.

'You fainted,' replied Harry. 'They siphoned off the fluid. You're in the room next to the operating theatre.'

The wooden floor was hurting Harry's side, so he sat up cross-legged. Miklós lay in silence for a long time. Then he mumbled, 'You know what, Harry? I'll develop gills. They won't get the better of me.'

'Who won't?'

'No one will. No one knows just how stubborn I can be.'

'I envy you. You're so strong.'

'You'll be all right too. I know it. Your slug will turn into a pine tree rising to the sky. And then there'll be no stopping you.'

Harry was rocking back and forth, thinking about what Miklós had said. 'Are you sure?'

'Test my sword, ladies!' said my father, trying to smile, and remembering what he had written to Lili.

> Now for a strange question. How are you placed in the love department? Is that irritatingly indiscreet of me?

~

One afternoon, having asked a nurse where to find the best greengrocer in Eksjö, Sára took the lift to the ground floor and escaped from the hospital. In the persistent drizzle she made a dash for the old town, which still had its charms. Fate rewarded her: the only thing in the grocer's window was a wicker basket, and in the basket were several fleshy green peppers. Sára stared at them in amazement while she got her breath back. Then, fishing her small change from her pocket, she sauntered in.

The answer to your 'strange' question is simple: I've
had a few boyfriends. Does that mean I've had a lot or
just one special one? You'll have to guess!

~

Harry was the dandy of the barracks. He loved swaggering
around like some grand seducer, and his enigmatic smile suggested that he'd already broken the hearts of umpteen women.
Naturally, Miklós was the only one who knew about his little
'problem'.

Then someone discovered that Harry kept a precious,
shapely bottle of cologne hidden under his mattress. No one
knew where he'd got it from but sometimes, before he walked
into town, the whole barracks was filled with the pungent scent
of lavender. One evening, when Harry was about to set out on
one of his jaunts, he discovered the bottle was missing.

Soon it was flying through the air and, desperate to get it
back, Harry was rushing in every direction. The men would
wait for him to come close, and then throw the bottle to each
other over his head. Tiring of that game, they unscrewed the
top and splashed each other with the scent. Harry, tears in his
eyes, pleaded with them. 'I bought it on borrowed money,' he
shouted.

My fellow patients are horrible. That's why this letter
is such a mess. Hungarians, the lot of them! And
there's such chaos in here that I can't even write.

They've drenched the place in the cologne belonging
to our resident Don Juan. Some of it even landed on
my writing paper. We're in such high spirits it's almost
dangerous. Harry and I may have to break out and
trek across the country to see you and your friends.

~

When Sára got back from her expedition to the old town Lili
was asleep. This was a stroke of luck. She delicately laid the two
peppers on the pillow next to Lili's cheek.

> How thrilling, dear Miklós, that you and your friend
> may come and visit us.

~

Miklós and Harry often exercised by striding around the hospital
grounds. Now that a trip to Eksjö might be on the cards—Miklós
was cooking up some story about a family reunion—Harry was
full of curiosity. He was determined to get his own penfriend, or
at least to make certain of going on the visit with Miklós. 'How
many kilometres is it exactly?' he enquired.

'Almost three hundred.'

'Two days there, two days back. We won't get permission.'

Miklós led the way, keeping his eyes on the path.

'Yes, we will.'

Harry felt this was the time to banish all doubt about his

virility. 'I'm in much better shape. Every morning I wake up with a stiff, like this!' he said, showing the length with his hands.

But Miklós didn't react.

> Whatever happens, don't forget that I'm your cousin and Harry is Sára's uncle. I have to warn you, though, that at the station, yes, right there at the station, you'll be getting a kiss from your cousin. We must keep up appearances!
>
> I send you a friendly handshake plus a kiss from your cousin, Miklós.

~

One rare sunny morning in Eksjö, the door swung open and there stood a grinning, chubby Judit Gold! She dropped her belongings and threw her arms out wide. 'Dr Svensson gave me a referral too. Severe anaemia. We can all be together!'

Sára flew over to Judit and they hugged each other. Lili clambered out of bed, though it was strictly forbidden, and, linking arms, the three of them danced in front of the window. Then they sat on Lili's bed.

'Does he still write to you?' asked Judit, taking Lili's hand in hers.

Lili waited a moment. She had recently learned the subtle advantage of pausing for effect. She stood up and in a dramatic gesture pulled open the drawer of her bedside table. She took out a sheaf of letters and held it high.

'Eight!'

Judit applauded. 'How industrious of him.'

Sára patted Judit on the knee. 'You should see how clever he is! And a socialist, too.'

That was a little too much for Judit, who pulled a face. 'Ugh, I hate socialists.'

'Lili doesn't.'

Judit took the letters out of Lili's hands and smelled them. 'Are you sure he's not married?'

Lili was taken aback. Why did she have to smell them? 'Dead sure.'

'We ought to check him out somehow. You know, I've been burnt so many times.'

Judit was at least ten years older than the other two, and she knew more about men. Lili took the letters from her, slipped off the rubber band and picked up the top one.

'Listen to what he says: "I've got good news for you. We can send cables to Hungary now. But you have to use special forms. You can get them either from the consulate or from the Red Cross in Stockholm. Each form can fit twenty-five words." How about that?'

This was wonderful to hear. They thought about it for a while. Lili lay back in her bed, put the letters on her stomach and stared at the ceiling. 'I haven't heard anything from Mama. Or Papa. I can't bear it. Aren't you worried too?'

The girls avoided each other's eyes.

~

Autumn had by now slunk across the island of Gotland too. It was a bleak overcast day when Dr Lindholm summoned the inhabitants of the barracks together at noon. He briskly gave them the good news that none of them remained infectious. And that early the following morning the Hungarian patients were being transferred to a temporary hospital in Avesta, north of Stockholm. Dr Lindholm would be travelling with them.

~

Avesta was a few hundred kilometres away. After a day and a half of chugging along on steam trains they arrived. At first sight, their new rehabilitation camp was a shock. Situated in the middle of thick forest, seven kilometres from the town, it was surrounded by a wire fence and, worst of all, a tall chimney rose from its centre.

They were housed in brick barracks. They might have settled in better if the weather had not been so terrible. The wind always blew in Avesta. Everything was covered in frost, and the sun, the colour of an overripe orange, never peeped out for more than a few minutes.

Outside their window was a small concrete courtyard full

of weeds. Its long wooden table and benches gave it a certain spartan charm. The convalescents sat here in the evenings wrapped up in blankets.

Dr Lindholm had arranged for a Hungarian newspaper to be delivered every few days, even if it was three weeks old. The men instantly tore the shoddily printed paper into four parts. Huddled in groups, they devoured every word. A single light bulb swung overhead. Then they swapped pages in the pale light, their mouths moving soundlessly. In spirit they were far away.

THE REBUILT 250-HORSEPOWER SCREW STEAMER SETS OUT ON ITS MAIDEN VOYAGE

SOVIET PAINTER ALEXANDR GERASIMOV IS CELEBRATED IN THE HOTEL GELLÉRT

THE TOWN OF KECSKEMÉT RECEIVES A GIFT OF 300 PAIRS OF OXEN FROM THE OCCUPYING RUSSIAN FORCES

BICYCLE RACE IN SZEGED

SHOOTING STARTS ON THE FILM *THE TEACHER*

Just imagine! We got hold of an August edition of *Kossuth's People*. We even read all the ads. The theatres back home are full. A four-page newspaper costs two pengő, a kilo of flour fourteen. The people's court is sentencing members of the Arrow Cross Party one after the other. There are lots of new street names. Mussolini Square is now Marx Square. The

whole country is full of hope. People want to work.
Teachers have to attend re-education courses. The
first lecture was given by party boss Mátyás Rákosi.
But I'm sure you're sick of politics.

~

The tiny X-ray room in Avesta was no different from the one
in Lärbro. Except perhaps for the hairline crack that ran the
length of the ceiling. It was a symbol of something and it gave
Miklós a feeling of hope. In this room he once again pressed
his sunken chest and narrow shoulders up against the machine.
And once again it gave out a high thin beep when the X-ray
was done. Miklós always covered his eyes when the door opened
and light streamed into the darkness. And it was always Dr
Lindholm who stood in the doorway in his radiation-proof
leather apron.

The X-rays were read the following day. Miklós entered Dr
Lindholm's office and sat down in front of the desk. He leaned
back until the front legs of his chair rose into the air. It was to
become an annoying habit in Avesta. He had made a bet with
himself. If something of vital importance was being discussed,
he would pivot on his chair like a naughty child—all the while
concentrating like mad.

'The X-rays came out well. Sharp, easy to read,' Dr Lindholm
said, looking into my father's eyes.

'Any change?'

'I can give no encouraging.'

Miklós let the chair drop back on all four legs.

'And forget about going to Eksjö. Is too far away from Avesta. God knows how long to get there.'

'I only want three days.'

'You have always fever at dawn. There are no miracles.'

Miklós had his own thermometer. Each morning, at half past four on the dot, an inner alarm clock woke him up. The mercury always reached the same point. Thirty-eight point two. No more, no less.

'This is not about me. My cousin is lonely and depressed. It would mean the world to her.'

Dr Lindholm gave him a thoughtful glance. He and Márta, who was now head nurse in their section in Avesta, had settled into their new home. He decided to invite Miklós, who got on well with his wife, for supper. Perhaps over a family meal he could dissuade this charming and stubborn young man from his crazy scheme.

~

The Lindholms' house was next to the railway line. Trains regularly shrieked past the window. Miklós dressed for the occasion, having borrowed a jacket and tie, but he felt ill at ease. At the beginning, conversation was awkward. Márta dished out the stuffed cabbage. Dr Lindholm tucked his napkin into his shirt.

'Márta cook this dish especially for you. Hungarian, she tell me.'

There was the banshee noise of a passing train.

'It's one of my favourites,' replied Miklós when it was quiet again. He broke a crust of bread and carefully gathered up the crumbs.

Márta smacked his hand. 'If you don't stop cleaning up, I'll send you out to wash the dishes.'

He blushed. For a while they blew on the hot cabbage in silence.

Miklós started to cough. After he caught his breath, he said, 'Dr Lindholm speaks beautiful Hungarian.'

'I won on that score. In everything else Erik is the boss,' said Márta, smiling at her husband.

They continued to eat in silence. Fatty cabbage juice started to trickle down Miklós's chin. Márta handed him a napkin. He wiped his mouth in embarrassment.

'Can I ask you how you two met?'

Márta, who could barely reach the table from her chair, stretched her hand out between the glasses and laid it on Lindholm's arm. 'Can I tell him?'

Dr Lindholm nodded.

'It was ten years ago. A delegation of Swedish doctors came to visit the Rókus Hospital in Budapest. None of them was tall. I was the head nurse there,' Márta said, then stopped.

Dr Lindholm sipped his wine. He was not going to help her out.

'Since I was a teenager people have always teased me. Look at me, Miklós, you can see why, can't you? If I was asked to open a window, I had to get someone in the class to do it for me. When I was sixteen I told my mother that, as soon as I could, I would move to Sweden and find a husband. So I started learning Swedish.'

A passenger train clattered past. It felt as if it had passed between them and the plates.

'Why Sweden?'

'Is common knowledge that very short men live here,' Dr Lindholm retorted.

It was five seconds before Miklós dared to laugh. It was as if a plug had been pulled out: now the conversation flowed.

'By 1935 I could speak Swedish fluently. By coincidence Dr Lindholm had had enough of his previous wife. She was a giant—six foot. That's right, isn't it, Erik?'

Dr Lindholm nodded gravely.

'What was I to do? One evening I seduced him. In the hospital. Next to the operating theatre. I haven't left anything out, have I, Erik? Now it's your turn, Miklós. Did you tell the girl in Eksjö about your condition?'

My father, who until now had been preoccupied with his napkin, picked up his knife and fork and started to wolf down the cabbage. 'More or less.'

'Erik and I differ on this. I think you should go. To cheer up your … cousin. And yourself.'

Dr Lindholm sighed and poured more wine into everybody's

glasses. 'Last week I receive letter from my colleague who work in Ädelfors,' he said. He jumped up and hurried into the other room. A moment later he returned clutching a sheet of paper.

'I read you parts, Miklós. There is women's hospital in Ädelfors, a rehabilitation centre for four hundred inmates. Well, about fifty girls were transferred to different hospital with stricter regime. What you think reason?' he asked, brandishing the letter.

Miklós shrugged. Lindholm didn't wait for the answer.

'Their loose life. I read it to you. Listen. "The girls received men in their bedrooms and in clearings in the nearby forest."'

No one had anything to say.

After a while the tiny Márta asked, 'Were they Hungarian girls?'

'I don't know.'

But Miklós knew the answer. 'They were spoilt upper-class girls!' he announced triumphantly.

Márta put down her fork in alarm. 'What's that supposed to mean, Miklós?'

My father was at last on familiar ground. He intended to enjoy himself. The dusty world of the past had been blown away by the fresh wind of socialism.

'Women like that adhere to a certain type of morality. They smoke, wear nylon stockings and chatter away about superficial things. *While from the depths not a word.*' Miklós couldn't resist quoting the poetry of Attila József.

'I'm not sure about that,' said Dr Lindholm. 'All I know, opportunity makes a thief.'

But Miklós was not so easily deterred. 'There's only one way to cure those bourgeois morals.'

'And that is?'

'By building a new world! From the foundations.'

From that point on, the supper was overwhelmed by my father's rousing manifesto in praise of the redeeming trinity of *liberté, égalité, fraternité*. He didn't even notice that they had polished off the dessert.

After midnight Dr Lindholm's car swung into the entrance of the hospital. Miklós clambered out and waved goodbye. He was buoyant, full of hope that he would soon be off to Eksjö. As soon as he got back to his barracks, he lit a candle, crouched down at his bed and excitedly condensed his world-saving ideology into a four-page letter.

> It will make me happy if you write and tell me what
> you think about all this. I'm especially interested
> because you are middle class, and probably look
> at this question from the point of view of the
> bourgeoisie.

Four

IN THE third week of October, Dr Svensson allowed Lili to get up. She forlornly roamed the tiled corridors of the hospital. The acrid smell of disinfectant mingled with the stench of gutted fish. The women's section was on the third floor, but otherwise the place seemed to be full of surly Swedish soldiers.

Lili was about to spend her first Sunday with the Björkmans. Two months earlier, at Smålandsstenar, each of the Hungarian girls had been introduced to a Swedish family who would help them find their feet. Sven Björkman ran a small stationery shop. He and his family were practising Catholics.

Lili wasn't assigned to the Björkmans by chance. It was five months since her 'betrayal'. In May, just after the war ended, when she regained consciousness in a hospital in the town of Belsen after being rescued from the concentration camp, she immediately renounced her Jewish faith. The truth is that she chose Catholicism quite randomly. But it meant that later, thanks to the thoroughness and the sensitivity of the Swedish authorities, the Björkman family was chosen to support her.

Björkman, his wife and their two sons made the long drive to Eksjö at dawn the next Sunday. They waited for Lili at the hospital entrance, hugged her joyfully on seeing her again, and then took her straight to mass in Smålandsstenar.

The Björkman family sat in the third pew of the simple but spacious church. And the convalescent Hungarian girl, Lili Reich, sat with them. Their radiant faces turned towards the pulpit. Lili understood only a few words of Swedish so the sermon washed over her with the same solemnity as the organ fugue that followed it. Then she, too, kneeled in the line before the young priest with the piercing blue eyes, so he could place a wafer on her tongue.

Dear Miklós,

I'd like to ask you not to hurry so much next time you write, but rather to think over what you're writing and to whom. Our relationship isn't that close. Mind what you say to me! Yes, I'm a typical bourgeois girl. And if, among four hundred girls, 'about fifty' fit your description of them, why should you be surprised?

~

That same Sunday morning Miklós and Harry were sitting in front of a few scones and glasses of soda water in the Avesta canteen. They should have been celebrating the fact that they had the place to themselves, but Miklós was in such a bad mood that he didn't even notice.

'I've ruined it,' he muttered.

Harry waved him down. 'Of course you haven't. She'll calm down.'

'Never. I've got a feeling.'

'Then you can write to someone else.'

Miklós looked up, shocked. 'There isn't anyone else. It's either her or I die.' How could Harry be so insensitive?

Harry burst out laughing. 'Words, just words?'

Miklós dipped his finger in the glass of water and wrote 'LILI' on the wooden table. 'This'll dry up too,' he said sadly.

'Send her one of your poems!'

'Too late.'

'I don't like sorrowful Jews,' said Harry, getting up. 'I'll find you something sweet. I'll bribe someone or steal something for you. But wipe that glum look off your face.'

Harry crossed the dreary hall to the swing door and entered the kitchen. There was no one there either. He opened cupboards until he found a jar of honey buried deep in one of them.

He hurried back in triumph. 'No spoon. You'll have to dip your finger in, like this.'

My father was staring at the table. The stem of the second 'L' was still visible.

'Right.' Harry sucked his finger. 'Have you got paper and a pencil? I'll dictate.'

'What?' asked Miklós, looking up at last.

'A letter. To her. Are you ready?' He dipped his finger in the honey.

Puzzled, Miklós took some paper and a pencil out of his pocket. Harry's cheerfulness had managed to strike a tiny crack in the armour of his despair.

'Dear Lili,' Harry dictated, licking his finger, 'I have to tell you that I despise and deride those stupid women who are ashamed to talk about such things—'

Miklós slammed down his pencil. 'This is lunacy! You want me to send this to Lili?'

'You've been writing to each other for a month now. It's high time you became more intimate with her. I'm an outsider, I can gauge things better.'

~

The following Sunday, after Sven Björkman had said grace, and the two Björkman boys had more or less settled down, Mrs Björkman began ladling out the soup with her usual precision.

'Where have you hidden your crucifix, Lili?' Björkman asked, without so much as a glance at Lili.

Either he spoke little German or he wanted to test Lili's

knowledge of Swedish. When she looked at him blankly, he repeated the question, in Swedish, and pointed to the crucifix round his own neck.

Lili blushed. She fished the little silver cross out of her pocket and put it round her neck.

'Why did you take it off?' he asked, looking at her pleasantly. 'We gave it to you for you to wear. Always.'

The reproach was clear. The meal passed without further conversation.

> The tone and content of your last letter were rather strange but you seem like a kind man, so I'll answer this one too. On the other hand, I'm not sure that a 'bourgeois' girl like me is the right friend for you. This time I think you went too far.

~

It was dawn. Miklós felt for the thermometer in the drawer of his bedside table, and with his eyes still shut he stuck it in his mouth. Then he counted to 130. He opened his eyes for a split second: there was no need for him to study the delicate markings in detail. The fever, as stealthy as a thief, crept up, stole his confidence, and then vanished in the half-light of dawn. He put the thermometer in the drawer again, turned over and went back to sleep.

When he got up at eight o'clock his temperature was normal.

Dear Lili,

What a fool I am! I'm sorry. Why do I bother you with all my stupid thoughts? I send you a warm handshake.

Miklós

P.S.: Is that still allowed?

~

It took two days for a letter to arrive by Swedish mail train. When Miklós's apology arrived, Lili and Sára were huddled on Lili's bed.

'"P.S. Is that still allowed?"'

'Now you should forgive him,' said Sára after some thought.

'I already have.'

Lili scrambled across the bed and took an envelope from her bedside table.

'I purposely left it open,' she said as she searched for the bit she wanted to show Sára. 'Here it is: "Yes, Miklós, you really are a fool! But if you behave yourself we can be friends again."' She gave Sára a jubilant look.

'Men!' said Sára, smiling.

~

Four bicycles were kept in the entrance to Avesta, so patients could ride from the forest to the town. Now that the weather had turned cold and even the midday sunshine didn't melt the snow on the fir trees, Miklós and Harry had to rug up to prevent their ears and hands from freezing on the hour-long ride.

Even so, it took a long time, as they sat waiting at the post office, for the feeling to return to their fingers, though they tried to keep them warm under their thighs.

Miklós was anxious. From where they sat he could see the glass doors of the three telephone booths, which at that moment were all occupied. He was beside himself. It was his turn next.

After what seemed forever one of the booths became vacant. At the counter, an operator lifted the receiver to her ear. She looked at Miklós, said something into the phone and waved at him. He stood up and staggered into the vacant booth.

~

Judit Gold dashed up the stairs at full speed, practically knocking over the nurses and doctors hurrying in the opposite direction. Lili and Sára were reading in the open window of the ward. Judit stormed through the door. 'Lili! Lili!' she shouted. 'You've got a phone call!'

Lili gaped at her, not understanding.

'Hurry! Miklós is on the phone!'

Lili turned red and leapt off the windowsill. She flew downstairs to the basement, where a telephone room had been set up for patients. A nurse was on her way out of the room, and she looked at Lili in surprise. Lili saw the receiver lying on the table. She made herself slow down. She touched the receiver gingerly, and cautiously lifted it to her ear. 'It's me.'

In the post office Miklós gave a small cough, but his voice still came out an octave higher than its usual baritone. 'You sound exactly the way I imagined you would,' he managed to say. 'How mystical!'

'I'm out of breath. I ran. There's just one telephone, in the main building, and we ... '

Miklós started to babble. 'Catch your breath. I'll do the talking, all right? Remember I told you how you can already send cables home? I'm calling because—just imagine—now we can send airmail letters too, via London or Prague. At last you can find your mother! Isn't it great! I thought I'd call and tell you right away.'

'Oh dear.'

'Did I say something wrong?'

Lili was clutching the receiver so tightly that her fingers had turned white. 'Mama ... I don't know ... I don't know her address ... She had to leave our old flat and move to the ghetto ... and now I don't know where she is living.'

Miklós's voice recovered its silky tone. 'Oh, I'm a fool. Of course you don't! But we can place a notice in a newspaper. We'll send her a message through *Világosság*. Everyone reads that. I've got a bit of money saved up. I'll arrange it.'

Lili was surprised. There was no way he could afford to do that on five kronor a week.

'How have you been able to save any money?'

'Didn't I tell you, my darling? Oh, sorry, have I gone too far? I'm sorry, Lili.'

Lili blushed furiously. Now her temperature had shot up. 'I wish I could see you.'

The post office felt like a palace to Miklós. Thrilled, he punched the air with his fist, signalling to Harry through the glass. 'Well, it's like this, what if I had a Cuban uncle ... but that's a long story, I'll put it in a letter.'

No one spoke for a while. They pressed the receivers tightly to their ears.

'How are you?' Lili started up again. 'Your health, I mean.'

'Me? I'm fine. All my tests are negative. There was a tiny spot on my left lung. Some fluid. A touch of pleurisy. But not serious. I'm more or less in the middle of my treatment. And you?'

'I'm fine, too. Nothing hurts. I have to take iron tablets.'

'Have you got a temperature?' Miklós asked.

'Very slight. A kidney infection. Nothing to worry about. I've got a good appetite. I'm so looking forward to seeing you ... seeing you both,' said Lili.

'Yes. I'm working on it. But in the meantime I've written you a poem.'

'Me?' Lili blushed again.

Miklós closed his eyes. 'Shall I recite it?'

'You know it by heart?'

'Of course.'

He had to think quickly. The truth was that he had already

written six poems for Lili, to Lili. Now he had to choose one. 'The title is "Lili". You still there?'

'Yes.'

Miklós leaned against the booth wall. He kept his eyes closed.

> *I stepped on an icy puddle*
> *the rime crunched under me.*
> *If you touch my heart, beware,*
> *a single move will be*
> *enough to crack apart*
> *my secret frozen sea.*

'Are you still there?'

Lili held her breath.

He couldn't hear her, but he could sense her presence.

'Yes.'

Miklós was frightened by something, too, or perhaps he was just hoarse. The distance made the receiver hiss, and the words of the poem sounded like breaking waves. 'I'll go on then,' he said.

> *So come to me gently,*
> *with the smiles that we lost.*
> *Seek out the places*
> *where pain has chilled to frost*
> *so the warmth of your caress*
> *melts to dew within my chest.*

Five

THE GROUND-FLOOR meeting room, which the hospital in Eksjö had made available to the Red Cross, was tiny and embarrassingly bare. It had no window. There was just room for a desk and a bentwood chair for visitors.

Madame Ann-Marie Arvidsson was the local Red Cross representative. She sharpened her pencil after almost every sentence she wrote. She spoke German slowly, enunciating every syllable to make it easier for Lili to understand the finer points. And she was set on explaining everything to this charming Hungarian girl. Even things that were out of her hands.

Such as the risk Sweden had taken by allowing in so many sick people. Such as the fact that the International Red Cross never had enough money, because all sorts of unforeseeable expenses were always cropping up. She didn't even get to the question of accommodation. The main thing was, like it or not, she couldn't support this kind of private initiative.

'You ought to know, Lili, I don't agree with this type of visit even in principle.'

Lili tried again. 'Just a few days. What harm will that do anyone?'

'It won't do any harm. But what would be the point? To come from the other side of the country. That's a lot of money. And once the men are here? Among three hundred patients. This is a hospital, not a hotel! Have you considered that, Lili?'

'I haven't seen them for a year and a half.' She gave the woman an imploring look.

Madame Arvidsson thought she saw a speck of dust on the immaculate surface of the desk. She wiped it off. 'Let's say I give permission. What will your relatives eat? The Red Cross has no funds for extra food.'

'Something. Anything.'

'You are not facing facts, Lili. These men are patients too. I can't even imagine how they'll buy the tickets for the train.'

'We've got a Cuban relative.'

Ann-Marie Arvidsson raised an eyebrow. She jotted down a few words, then sharpened her pencil. 'And this relative is financing the visit, all the way from Cuba?'

Lili looked deep into Madame Arvidsson's eyes. 'We're a loving family ... '

This, at last, made Madame Arvidsson laugh. 'I admire your determination. I'll try to do something. But I can't make any promises.'

Lili got up, leaned awkwardly over the desk and gave Madame Ann-Marie Arvidsson a kiss. Then she ran out of the room, knocking over her chair on the way.

Ann-Marie Arvidsson got up, set the chair on its legs, took out her handkerchief and wiped all trace of the kiss off her cheek.

~

A few days later Rabbi Emil Kronheim climbed briskly onto a train in Stockholm. The rabbi was an ascetic figure, small and thin, in an old grey suit. His hair was like a haystack. Ever since the Swedish government had called on him to give moral support to his fellow Jews in these hard times, his name and address had been pinned on the noticeboard of every rehabilitation centre in Sweden.

He travelled up and down the country for three weeks of each month. Sometimes he talked to people in groups. Other times he would listen to a single person for hours on end, hardly moving, giving strength with just the bat of an eyelid, until they were engulfed by the early evening twilight. He never grew tired.

His one excess was herring. It was almost comical. He couldn't resist pickled herring. Even on the train, reading the newspaper, while the snow-covered countryside raced past, he ate pieces of herring out of greasy paper.

At the station in Eksjö he clambered out of his carriage. It was pouring. He hurried across the wet platform.

According to his information there were three young Hungarian women in the hospital. A few days ago he had received a letter from one of them. A single soul is a soul. Without a moment's hesitation he had set out on the mind-numbing journey from Stockholm.

Now he was sitting in the same windowless room that had confined Madame Ann-Marie Arvidsson. He was concentrating on a fly that was crawling around the desk between the pencils, the sharpener.

There was a knock. Judit Gold stuck her head round the door. 'Can I come in?'

The rabbi smiled. 'Just as I imagined you. You see, dear—'

'I'm Judit Gold.'

'You see, dear Judit Gold, on the basis of your handwriting I formed a mental picture of you. Now comes my pat on the back: I've scored a bullseye. Incidentally the world is built on this kind of presentiment. Before the Battle of Waterloo, Napoleon … Oh, you look so pale. Can I get you some water?'

There was a jug on the desk. Rabbi Kronheim filled a glass.

Judit Gold drank greedily, then sat down. She spoke in a whisper. 'I'm ashamed of myself.'

'So am I. We all are. And we've reason to be. What's the reason for your shame, Judit?'

'I'm ashamed of writing you that letter. And of being forced to tell tales.'

'Don't tell tales then! Forget the whole thing.'

'I can't.'

'Of course you can. Shrug it off and throw what you wanted to tell me into the bin. Don't give it another thought. Forget it. Let's talk about something else. Let's talk about flies, for example. What's your attitude to flies?'

Emil Kronheim pointed to the fly buzzing over the desk.

'They disgust me.'

'You want to be careful with disgust. It can easily turn into hatred. And right after that comes conflict. Later, it becomes ideology. And in the end you'll be pursuing flies all your life.'

Judit couldn't take her eyes off the fly that had now landed on the rim of her glass. 'I've got a friend,' she said.

Judit paused. She was in need of a question or a gesture, but Kronheim seemed interested only in the fly, the crazy, fidgety fly.

She had to start somewhere. 'It's about my friend Lili. She's eighteen. Inexperienced and naïve.'

The rabbi shut his eyes. Was he listening at all?

'She has been completely ensnared by a man from Gotland. Well, he has now been transferred to Avesta. I can't stand by and do nothing. I can't bear seeing Lili getting all worked up about him. There's no way I can keep calm or stay out of this.'

The rabbi, who had been so chatty to start with, was now sitting still, his eyes closed. Had he fallen asleep?

Judit started crying. 'She is my best friend. I've grown to

love her. She was skin and bone when she arrived. She was so down. So alone. Then she started writing letters to this good-for-nothing. He's a gangster. He promises her everything under the sun. Right now he wants to come and visit her in the hospital. Sorry, I'm not making any sense. All I know is that Lili's too young.'

Judit felt that she had lost the thread. She should tell the story from the beginning. Tell him why she was anxious and why her fears were real. But, instead of helping her out, the rabbi was confusing her. He sat there with his eyes closed, his back straight. He wasn't paying attention.

A minute passed. Then Rabbi Kronheim ran his fingers through his untidy hair. So he hadn't been asleep.

Judit snivelled and sniffed. 'I've lived through so much horror. I've given up so many times. But I'm alive. I'm still here. And Lili is so young.'

Emil Kronheim put his hand in his pocket. 'I always have a clean handkerchief on me for such occasions. Here you are.'

~

Around this time Miklós began to figure out how he could trick fate. He had no illusions about his looks. Even though he now weighed fifty kilos, and the nasty warts were starting to disappear, he remained self-conscious.

Dr Lindholm was surprised by his request, but for once it wasn't about going to Eksjö, and it was something that would make Miklós happy, so he agreed right away. He went over to the cupboard and took out a small camera. Then he got a roll of film out of his desk drawer. He handed them both to Miklós, who was standing in the middle of the room, beaming.

Miklós, Harry and Tibor Hirsch headed across to a spacious, breezy tract of land between the barracks where hundred-year-old pine trees rose up high. Miklós solemnly handed the camera to Tibor, who at over fifty was the oldest of the patients. His hair didn't seem to want to grow; irregular-shaped purple patches could be seen on his scalp.

'You were a photographer,' Miklós said, looking at him. 'I trust you. My life's in your hands.'

Hirsch spent a long time examining the camera. 'I know this type. It'll be perfect, I promise.'

Miklós interrupted. 'No, it shouldn't be perfect.'

'What?'

'It should be fuzzy. That's what I want.'

Hirsch looked puzzled.

'That's why I asked you. Because you know what you're doing.'

'Only to a point. I'm an electronic radio technician and photographer's assistant. Or used to be. What *do* you want?'

Miklós now pointed at Harry. 'We both should be in the picture. Harry and me. Harry should be in focus. I should be blurred, somewhere in the background. Could you do that?'

'That's nuts!' Hirsch protested. 'Why on earth do you want to be out of focus?'

'Never you mind. Can you do it?'

Tibor Hirsch, electronic radio technician and photographer's assistant, hesitated. But Miklós was his friend, and was giving him begging looks, so he put aside his professional pride.

Within five minutes he had worked out how to take a photograph in which my father would be more or less unrecognisable. He posed Harry in the foreground. In half-profile, at the most flattering angle. A watery sun came out for the briefest moment. Hirsch positioned them with backlight for an artistic feel. He instructed Miklós to run up and down a few metres behind Harry. Hirsch took several shots while Miklós ran.

> Dear Lili,
> What a sorceress you are! You enchanted me
> on the telephone. Now I'm even more keen to see
> whether you are as I imagine you from your letters.
> There'll be trouble if you aren't, but even more
> trouble if you are. I've found a photo of myself and
> Harry, who's standing in the front. Granted I look like
> I've been crushed by some sort of Cyclops and I'm in
> a hurry to get to the smallest room in the house—but
> I'm sending it anyway.

~

An artificial palm with lush tropical foliage stood in front of an alcove window on the third-floor corridor of the Eksjö hospital. The three girls sat there, hidden from sight.

Lili was examining the photograph with a magnifying glass. She handed it to Sára and Judit. There was nothing wrong with their eyesight. But was that indistinct shape running away behind Harry's back, that almost unidentifiable figure, Miklós?

A shadow loomed over them. 'Ah ha, so that's why you needed my magnifier.'

The three girls jumped as one. Dr Svensson pointed to the photo. 'Men? Hungarians?'

Lili held out the photo in embarrassment. 'It's my cousin.'

Svensson took a good look. 'Handsome. An open face.'

Lili hesitated, but then she pointed at the hazy figure in the background. 'That's him, the one who seems to be running away.'

Dr Svensson lifted the photograph close to his eyes, trying to identify the young man loping out of the frame, but it was hopeless. 'I thought he was in the picture by mistake. How mysterious.'

Miklós's idea was a success. The mysterious figure had kept the promise of the future alive. The girls were laughing as Svensson handed back the photo in disappointment, and they returned his magnifying glass to him.

~

Now I'm going to be very cheeky, partly to you and partly to your friend Sára, to whom I send friendly greetings. You see, the thing is my friend Harry and I have acquired some rather ghastly muddy grey wool that nimble-fingered girls could conjure into passable sweaters. I'd like to ask you to do this for me—as soon as possible, of course.

At dawn the next day Lili sat up in bed and took a handkerchief from under her pillow. She folded it carefully and slipped it into the envelope on the bedside table.

Accept this trifle from me with love. I'm afraid it isn't quite as fine as I'd have liked, and since I haven't got an iron I had to press it under my pillow. How did you find the wool? By the way, it's getting colder and colder here, and since they haven't given us winter coats I always put on two cardigans if I go out for a walk.

At that moment Judit Gold stuck her head out from beneath her eiderdown and couldn't help but see Lili's look of peaceful happiness. She wasn't a bit pleased.

~

The mail was distributed every afternoon after the men had rested. It was usually Harry who went to get the letters from the caretaker's office and he would read out the names. 'Misi, Adolf, Litzman, Jenö Grieger, Jakobovits, Józsi, Spitz, Miklós ... '

My father got lots of letters, perhaps too many, but only one person's letters excited him. If he saw that Lili had written, he didn't have the patience to wait until he was back in bed, but greedily tore open the envelope on the way. Now a handkerchief slipped out onto the floor. He picked it up and smelled it over and over again.

> The fact that you pressed your handkerchief under your head just enhances its value for me ... Tell me, why is it that your letters bring me more and more joy?
> Sorry about the pencil, but I wanted to write back straight away and someone has taken the ink.
> I send you a long warm handshake.
> Miklós

~

In Eksjö there was a hall on the ground floor of the hospital, with a yellow-sided platform where a red velvet curtain could be let down to make a stage. When Sára had the idea that they should give an evening concert, she and the girls hoped that the women living on the third floor would come and listen to them. In actual fact almost all of the two hundred chairs were taken up by the soldiers. The occasional Swedish nurse, with her braided hair, crisply starched cloak and bonnet, was squeezed in between them like a raisin in a bun.

The girls performed four numbers. Sára sang, while Lili accompanied her on the harmonium. After three Hungarian songs, Sára began to sing the Swedish national anthem. She was halfway through it when the soldiers, unshaven and in pyjamas, kicked back their two hundred chairs, jumped to their feet and joined in, none of them in tune.

> These Swedes are starting to get on my nerves. They expect us to sing their praises all the time. I am indescribably homesick!

Six

KLÁRA KÖVES arrived unexpectedly on the midday train. She had just enough money to buy a rail ticket from her camp near Uppsala to Avesta. That didn't worry her in the slightest — she was convinced that Miklós would take care of everything.

At the station she arranged a lift in the mail van, which meant that she travelled the last few kilometres in style. It was early afternoon when she arrived at the hospital.

Klára was a large girl — her friends called her 'bear woman'. Her walk was more like a trudge. Her handshake was like a man's. A good part of her body was covered with a silky down that, in a certain light, looked a lot like fur. She had full, sensuous lips, a hooknose and a mop of unruly, dark brown hair.

She blew into the barracks like a whirlwind. 'I'm here, dear Miklós!' she shouted. 'I've come to you!'

The men froze. Miklós couldn't connect this hefty woman with the amusing, quick-witted girl he'd been exchanging letters with for the past two months. There must be some misunderstanding.

Klára Köves, it turned out, was one of nine women apart from Lili with whom my father had been corresponding after he sent out his initial batch of 117 letters. He couldn't help himself. He took great joy in the process of writing; it helped him understand things, and he was genuinely curious about the lives of these girls. Of course the letters he wrote to the nine women were nothing like his outpourings to Lili. He and Klára, for instance, merely shared their views on world issues. Klára had distributed socialist pamphlets during the war—that's how she got caught.

She made a beeline for my father, threw her arms around him and kissed him on the lips. 'I've been wanting to do that for weeks.'

The other men hadn't moved an inch. What an entrance! A real flesh-and-blood woman, all ninety kilos of her, had materialised before them, despite all the regulations, restrictions and prohibitions. Their dreams had become three-dimensional.

Miklós shuddered, trapped in Klára's embrace. 'Wanting to do what?'

'To tie our lives together! What else?'

At last Klára let go of him. She took some letters out of her handbag and threw them in the air. She turned to the other men, who by this time were scrambling off their beds and gathering around her. 'Do you know who you've got in your midst? A new Karl Marx! A new Friedrich Engels!'

The letters fell like confetti. The men were enchanted.

Miklós wanted to die on the spot.

Klára took his arm and led him out of the barracks. My father signalled urgently for Harry to follow. The three of them set off down the path that led to the forest. It was as if Klára had taken possession of Miklós, as if she were hugging a doll. Harry walked behind them, hoping for his turn. It began to drizzle.

'Look here, Klára,' said Miklós in what he hoped was a quiet but authoritative voice. 'You should know that I write to other girls. Lots of them, in fact.'

Klára laughed. 'Are you trying to make me jealous, sweetie?'

'Heavens, no. I just want to be clear with you. Letter-writing is our only entertainment. Not only for me, but for the whole barracks. But it may have caused you to misunderstand certain things.'

'Misunderstanding, my foot! I've fallen for you, honey! You're as clever as they get. I look up to you. You'll be my teacher and my lover! You're full of hang-ups, but I'll be your saviour.'

'I write tons of letters. I want you to know that.'

'All geniuses are complex. I had two before the war, so I know. You don't mind my coming clean, do you? I'm not a virgin. Hell, no! I'm many things, but no virgin. But I will be faithful to you, I can feel it. The thoughts and ideas you come up with! I know them by heart. Would you like to test me?'

She grabbed Miklós by the waist and covered his face with kisses. His glasses misted up. But even through the fog he could see the desperation in her eyes, her fear of rejection.

This unexpected discovery had a soothing effect on Miklós. 'Could I get a word in, please, Klára,' he said calmly.

'I just wanted to say,' Klára raced on, 'that I'll nurse you if you need it. I've completely recovered. I'm going to work! I'll move to be near you. Now, what did you want to tell me?'

Miklós extricated himself from Klára's grasp and turned to her. 'All right. Now for the facts. I write many letters, but only because I've got beautiful handwriting. People have noticed it. The men in the barracks take advantage of it, so to speak. Your letters, I'm afraid, were composed by Harry, not me. He dictated them to me because my writing is so much better than his. That's the sad truth. You fell for Harry's brain through me.'

Klára's eyes widened. She spun around to Harry. The drizzle was getting heavier. 'So it turns out you're my genius. Is that right, sweetheart?'

Harry cottoned on. He hoped his lonely preparation for the manly tasks that lay ahead would prove sufficient. 'He ... just did the writing,' he improvised, pointing to Miklós. 'The thoughts ... ' Harry gave his forehead a modest tap.

Klára looked from one man to the other. Miklós was short, wore glasses and had metal teeth. Harry was tall, with a neat moustache, and she must have detected the look of genuine desire in his eyes. She decided she was better off believing my father. She took Harry's arm.

'I'm going to get to know you, sweetheart. I don't give a damn about appearances. I don't care about the shape of a mouth, the colour of a man's eyes, whether he is handsome or not. It's the mind I go for, if you see what I mean. I get high on progressive, soaring ideas—I can't get enough of them.'

Harry turned the girl towards him, putting one hand on her ample bottom, and holding her chin in the other. 'I won't disappoint you,' he said boldly, and kissed her on the lips.

Miklós felt it was time to make his exit. At the end of the path he looked back and saw them locked in an embrace as they wandered towards the thick of the forest behind an increasingly heavy curtain of rain.

~

To atone for this episode with Klára, Miklós inflicted three days' penitence on himself. During this time he didn't write a word to Lili. On the fourth day, after getting the key from the caretaker, he ran a full bath of hot water in the only private bathroom on the grounds. It was in a separate building far from the barracks, so Miklós didn't bother to lock the door. He got into the bath, lit a cigarette and started bellowing out a workers' marching song. He wasn't exactly famous for his musical ear.

The door swung open. There was the tiny Márta, the head

nurse, trying to wave the thick smoke away. In shock, Miklós tried to cover his penis with his left hand.

Márta was in a rage. 'What do you think you're doing here, Miklós? Hiding away to smoke in secret? You ought to be ashamed! How old are you? You're behaving like a naughty schoolboy!'

My father dropped his cigarette in the water. He tried to wave the smoke away with his right arm but only managed to stir it up. He was shy about being naked and in his embarrassment covered himself with both hands.

Márta, in her huge nurse's cap, came right over to the bath. 'For you, Miklós, every cigarette means death,' she shouted. 'Each one costs you a day of life. Is it worth it? Answer me, you foolish man! Is it worth it?'

> Lili, my dear little friend,
>
> It's time for a confession. Not the one that I'm afraid to write down—but another one. I have to tell you that my ear for music is atrocious and my singing voice is deplorable. But, like all pacifists, I belt out marching songs at the top of my voice in the bath.
>
> It's terrible the way they watch over us here. We have to keep to a strict daily routine: with silent rest times and other fun and games. The chief tyrant is Márta, the Mickey Mouse–like head nurse, Dr Lindholm's Hungarian wife. She's always fussing around us.

The Mickey Mouse–like head nurse stomped across the garden. It was five minutes' walk to the caretaker's office, and Márta's anger grew with every step.

She practically tore the office door off its hinges.

Four days earlier, not least as a result of Klára Köves's patience, Harry had regained his lost masculinity. Although Klára went away slightly disappointed, they agreed to go on writing to each other. Harry, on the other hand, had worked up an appetite. This time it was big-boned Frida, the daytime caretaker—nicknamed 'baby elephant' by the men—who took his fancy. Harry meditated on the devious whims of his desire. It seemed that the days when only pale, wasp-waisted girls made an impression on him were inexplicably over.

When Márta appeared like an avenging angel in the caretaker's office, Frida and Harry (in his pyjamas) hadn't got past cuddling. But there was no time to break away from each other. Harry was grateful that the conversation took place in Swedish, of which he understood next to nothing.

'Did you sell Miklós cigarettes, Frida?'

Frida's plump arms held Harry in a tight clasp, which she didn't relax for a moment. 'Just two or three.'

'This is your last chance! If I catch you again I'll report you!' shouted Márta, and she turned on her heel, slamming the door behind her.

Of course, Frida was not just being generous by handing out cigarettes. The tiny mark-up she added went to supplement her meagre wages.

Honestly, I like a man who smokes, but you're an exception now. Please don't overdo it. I don't smoke, by the way.

~

Lili came into the ward like a sleepwalker. She sat down on her bed without a word, radiating despair. Judit, who was in bed reading *Tess of the d'Urbervilles* for the third time, closed the book and sat up.

Sára was pouring herself a cup of tea. She hurried over to Lili. 'Has anything happened? '

Lili, sitting there with drooping shoulders, didn't answer.

Sára put her hand on Lili's forehead. 'Your temperature's up again. Where's the thermometer?'

Judit got out of bed to get the thermometer, which they kept in a dish on the windowsill. Lili let the girls lift her arm then press it tightly to her side. They sat opposite her on the bed and waited.

The wind beat against the windowpane. Lili's soft voice sounded like a lone violin over the beat of its thrumming and creaking. 'Someone reported me.'

Judit straightened her back slightly. 'What?'

'I've just come from the Red Cross woman. She told me I'd been lying ... ' Lili stared at her slippers.

Silence. Sára remembered her name. 'Ann-Marie Arvids-son?' she queried.

' … That she knows Miklós isn't my cousin, he's an unknown letter-writer … '

Judit started to pace the room. 'Where did she get that from?'

' … and she's refusing to give permission. He can't come. Can't come!'

Sára kneeled down in front of Lili and kissed both her hands. 'We'll work something out. Get a hold on yourself, your temperature's up.'

Lili couldn't look up. 'She showed me a letter. It was written here, by one of us.'

'Who on earth?' Judit Gold was shouting now.

'She didn't say. She only told me it said that I had lied. Miklós isn't my cousin, as I had claimed, and that's why she is refusing permission for his visit.'

'We'll apply again,' Sára said. 'We'll go on putting in requests to receive visitors until they're sick of the sight of them.'

'Dearest Lili!' Judit collapsed at Lili's feet.

At last, Lili raised her head and looked at her friends. 'Who could hate me so much?'

Sára got up and took the thermometer from under Lili's arm. 'Thirty-nine point two. Get into bed this minute. We'll have to tell Svensson.'

The two girls laid Lili on her back and covered her with the eiderdown. She seemed incapable of moving on her own. They had to treat her like a baby.

'He's attracted to you,' remarked Judit by way of distraction.

Sára didn't understand at first. 'Who's attracted to Lili?'

'Svensson. You should see the looks he gives her.'

'Come off it!' Sára scoffed.

But Judit couldn't leave it alone. 'I'm never wrong in these matters.'

~

Miklós was standing on the iron girders of the bridge over the railway, staring at the tangle of tracks that snaked their way towards the horizon. The sky was steel grey.

A figure came into sight on the road. It was running. At the bridge it climbed the iron steps two at a time. Even so, Miklós only noticed it was Harry when he was standing beside him, puffing and panting.

'You going to jump?'

Miklós smiled. 'What makes you think that?'

'Your eyes. And the way you rushed off after we got the mail.'

A goods train pulled away below them. Its thick black smoke enveloped them like sorrow. Miklós grasped the bridge railings.

'No. I'm not going to jump.'

Harry leaned his elbows on the railings next to Miklós. They watched the departing train. When it had shrunk to a narrow streak in the distance, Miklós took a crumpled letter out of his pocket and handed it to Harry.

'I received this.'

Dear Sir,

In answer to your notice in today's *Szabad Nép*, I
regret to inform you that your mother and father were
the victims of a bombing raid on the Laxenburg camp
in Austria on 12 February 1945 ... I knew them very
well. It was me who guided them to the best place
in the camp, the Coffee Factory, where they would
be treated as humans and could get decent food and
accommodation. I'm extremely sorry that I am the
bearer of such sad news.

Andor Rózsa

Miklós had a confused and contradictory relationship with
his father. The owner of Gambrinus, the famous bookshop
in Debrecen, was a domineering character, prone to shouting and often to violence too. He didn't spare his wife—and
he didn't even need to be drunk to attack her. Unfortunately
he drank a lot. In spite of this, my grandmother often came
into the bookshop with a sandwich or an apple or a pear for
him.

My father always remembered a wonderful afternoon in
spring when, as a small boy, perched on the top rung of the
bookstore ladder, he became so engrossed in Alexei Tolstoy's
Peter the Great that, spellbound by the intrigues of the tsar's
court, his ears flaming red, he forgot all about the time.

In the evening his mother showed up, wearing a wide-
brimmed maroon hat. 'Miki, it's seven o'clock. You forgot to
come home for dinner. What are you reading?'

He looked up. The woman in the wide-brimmed maroon hat was familiar, but he couldn't quite place her.

Harry folded the letter and gave it back to Miklós without a word. They leaned against the railings and kept their eyes on the tracks. Some birds were circling overhead.

> Dear Miklós,
>   I am terribly sorry that the letter from Szolnok contained such dreadful news. I can't find the words to comfort you.

That afternoon Miklós rode a bike to the cemetery in Avesta. It started to rain. He wandered aimlessly along the headstones, sometimes leaning over an inscription to try to sound out the Swedish name.

> I'm sorry I'm so cold and that I'm taking this calamity so damn hard. Yesterday I went to the local cemetery. I hoped perhaps my loved ones, at the bottom of a mass grave, might be stirred by a cosmic memory … That's all.

~

Lili sat up in bed. It was late at night; the bulb above the door gave off a faint light. Her forehead was drenched in sweat. In the next bed Sára was lying uncovered in the foetal position. Lili slipped out of bed and kneeled beside her.

'Are you asleep?'

Sára turned over, as if she had been expecting her. 'I can't sleep either!' she whispered back.

In a moment Lili was lying beside her; she held Sára's hand. Together they watched the strange patterns on the ceiling made by the birch tree swaying in the wind.

'He got some news,' Lili said. 'About his parents. They were bombed.'

Sára's eyes flickered; she could see the letter lying on Lili's bedside table. 'Good God!'

'I've worked it out. It's 373 days since I had any news of my mother or my father.'

With wide eyes they stared at the windblown expressionist images above them.

Seven

THE MAIL van arrived in Avesta soon after lunch. A man in a fur-collared coat jumped out, went round to the back, propped the door open and sorted the letters. It usually took him a few minutes. Then he went over to the yellow letterbox—which looked more like a large suitcase—opened the door at the bottom with a key and scooped all the outgoing mail into an empty canvas sack. After that he tipped all the incoming mail into the letterbox.

It was part of my father's daily routine to monitor this tedious ritual from beginning to end. He had to be absolutely convinced that his letter—as a result of some insidious plot—didn't fall out of the canvas sack.

> Lili, dear,
>
> I'm sure that, if not today, then tomorrow, you will get good news. The letter is sitting in your father's pocket, and he's waiting for the chance to try out this more or less impossible feat of sending a letter to Sweden.

~

In the Eksjö hospital there was one place you could smoke without getting caught. It was a bathroom on the second floor, which was used every morning for taking showers, but was then empty until the evening.

Judit Gold smoked at least half a pack a day; that's where all her pocket money went. But Sára, too, smoked three cigarettes a day. Lili went along to keep them company.

Sára inhaled pensively. 'We could go into town this afternoon. I begged for permission,' she announced after a while.

Judit was sitting on the edge of the shower cubicle, her legs drawn up under her. 'What for?'

'We could get a photo of Lili taken for Miklós.'

Lili was shocked. 'God forbid! He'll take one look and flee.'

Judit could blow excellent smoke rings. 'That's a good idea. A photo of the three of us, so we can remember all this, later on.'

'Later on when?' asked Sára.

'One day, when we're somewhere else. When we're happy.' They meditated on this.

Then Lili said, 'I'm ugly. I don't want a photo.'

Sára smacked her hand. 'You're stupid, my friend, not ugly.'

Judit smiled enigmatically, her eyes following the smoke rings until they reached the ventilator.

~

In the post office Miklós leaned against the glass cubicle. He spoke in German to prevent any misunderstanding.

'I'd like to send a telegram.'

The clerk, who also wore glasses, gave him an encouraging look. 'Address?' she asked.

'Eksjö, Utlänningsläger, Korungsgården 7.'

She started to fill in the form. 'Message?'

'Two words. Two Hungarian words. I'll spell them.'

She took offence at that. 'Just say them, and I'll write them down.'

Miklós breathed in. He pronounced the words clearly, sylla-ble by syllable, in his melodious Hungarian. '*Sze-ret-lek, Li-li.*'

The girl shook her head. Quite a language. 'Spell them, please.'

Miklós went letter by letter. They progressed patiently. Then they got stuck. Whereupon Miklós reached under the glass, grabbed the girl's right hand and tried to guide her pencil.

It wasn't easy. At the capital L, the girl threw down her pencil and shoved the form across to my father. 'You write it.'

Miklós crossed out the mishmash and in his gorgeous, swirling script wrote in Hungarian: *I love you, Lili!*

He pushed the form back.

The clerk look nonplussed at the unfamiliar word. 'What does it mean?'

Miklós hesitated. 'Are you married, miss?'

'I'm engaged.'

'Oh! Congratulations. Well, it means … it means … '

He knew exactly how to translate into German the simplest and most beautiful declaration in the world. Even so he was reluctant to give himself away.

The girl was adding up. 'That'll be two kronor. So, are you going to tell me?'

Miklós suddenly lost his nerve. He turned pale. 'Give it back, please!' he shouted at her. 'Give it back!'

She shrugged and pushed the form across the counter. Miklós grabbed it and tore it to pieces. He felt utterly stupid and cowardly. How could he explain? Instead he grinned in embarrassment, nodded at the girl and fled the post office.

~

Late that evening the men, wrapped in their blankets, sat around the wooden table in the courtyard. Many of them had their eyes closed in the drowsy silence, or stared vacantly at the bare red-brick wall opposite.

Miklós was standing with his back against the wall, his eyes closed, as if he were asleep.

> I won't send any new poems now, just a sonnet. I've got bigger plans: I'm working out the plot for a novel. It's about twelve people—men, women, children, German, French and Hungarian Jews, cultured people and peasants—travelling in various railway freight wagons to a German concentration camp. From the security of life to certain death. That would be the first twelve chapters. The next twelve would describe the moment of liberation. It's still rather vague, but I'm very keen on the idea.

Pál Jakobovits—who couldn't have been much more than thirty, though his hands were constantly shaking and the doctors no longer comforted him by saying that one day he would get better—rocked back and forth mumbling: 'Dear God, hear my prayers. Dear God, send me a girl, a beautiful dark girl, let her be dark, a beautiful blonde girl, let her be blonde.'

Tibor Hirsch, radio technician and photographer's assistant, could only take so much. From the other end of the table he lashed out at Jakobovits. 'You make yourself ridiculous with that prayer.'

'I can pray for whatever I like.'

'You're not a kid any more, Jakobovits. You're over thirty.'

Jakobovits looked down. He grasped his left hand in his right as if somehow to stop the shaking. 'What's it got to do with you?'

'A man of thirty doesn't drool over women.'

'What does he do then?' Jakobovits yelled. 'Jerk off?'

'Don't be vulgar.'

Jakobovits sank his nails into his arm to overcome the cursed shaking. 'What does a man of thirty do?' he wailed. 'I'm waiting for the answer!'

'He stifles his desires. He asks for bromide. He waits his turn.'

Jakobovits thumped the table. 'I'm not waiting any more! I've waited enough.' He rushed into the barracks.

Standing at the wall, Miklós winced. He kept his eyes shut.

> Lili, dearest,
>   I would swear like hell if I weren't so ashamed.
> That helps me cope with things in the way crying
> helps girls. We're getting dreadfully out of hand here.
> I'd like to get hold of a book by August Bebel for you,
> *Woman and Socialism*. I hope I'll manage it.

~

Lili was curled up under her eiderdown, sobbing. It was past midnight. Sára woke up to the sound of her weeping and climbed out of bed. She lifted the eiderdown and started to stroke Lili's hair.

'Why are you crying?'

'No reason.'

'Did you have a bad dream?'

Sára got into bed beside Lili. They stared at the ceiling—this was becoming a habit. And then Judit Gold appeared hovering over them.

'Is there room for me too?'

The two girls made room, and Judit slipped in with them.

'Who is this Bebel fellow?' asked Lili.

Judit made a face. 'Some sort of writer.'

Sára sat up. This was her field. At times like this she acted like a schoolmistress and even wagged her index finger. 'Not "some sort of writer"! He was a wonderful person.'

'Apparently he wrote a book, *Woman and Socialism*.' Lili dried her eyes.

Judit, who was irritated by Sára's schoolmarmy manner, and in any case loathed left-wing thinking, couldn't help being sarcastic. 'Judging by the title I'll be rushing off to read it. Try stopping me!'

'It's Bebel's finest book. I learned a lot from it,' Sára insisted.

Judit gave Lili's arm a squeeze under the eiderdown. But since she never allowed herself to be beaten in literary debates she opened a new front. 'I'll bet your poet keeps stuffing your head with leftist ideas.'

'He wants to send me this book as soon as he can.'

'Learn chunks of it by heart. That'll impress him.'

Sára was still sitting up with her index finger raised. 'In *Woman and Socialism* Bebel claims that in a just society women have equal rights with men. In love, in war, in everything.'

'Bebel is a prat. He never had a wife.' Judit gave a scathing smile. 'No doubt he had syphilis.'

This made Sára see red. All sorts of retorts churned around in her head, but she couldn't choose the right one. So she lay down again.

> I can't wait to receive the book. Sára has read it
> already, but she'll happily read it again.

~

In Avesta the patients had been given two board games and a chess set. The instructions for the board games were in Swedish and the games themselves seemed rather primitive, so after trying to play them once the men gave up.

The chess set, on the other hand, they fought over. Litzman and Jakobovits were the best players. Apparently Litzman had been chess champion in his home town. He and Jakobovits played for money, and this gave them certain prerogatives over the board. Litzman gave a running commentary on the game for the benefit of the onlookers. He picked up the bishop, drew circles with it in the air and chanted, 'I'll ta-ha-ha-hake it! Che-he-heck!'

Jakobovits thought about this for long minutes.

In the tense silence, Hirsch's exclamation hit them like the celebratory chime of a bell. 'She's alive!' Hirsch was sitting up in bed waving a letter. 'She's alive! My wife is alive!'

FEVER AT DAWN

Everyone stared.

He stood up and looked around with a radiant face. 'Do you hear? She's alive!' He set out, marching between the beds, waving the letter like a flag above his head and shouting, 'She's alive! Alive! Alive!'

Harry was the first to join him. He fell in behind Hirsch with his hands on his shoulders, taking up the rhythm. They marched round and round between the beds, belting it out like the beat of a drum. 'She's alive! Alive! Alive!'

Then Fried, Grieger, Oblatt and Spitz joined in. There was no resisting the *joie de vivre* that swept them along, Miklós too, until all sixteen survivors were in a line. Hirsch led the way, holding the letter-flag up high, and behind him came the rest, Jakobovits and Litzman bringing up the rear.

They swirled around the room, finding different routes each time, like an endless snake. They clung to each other's shoulders and soon discovered they could tramp over everything, beds, tables, chairs—the main thing was not to break the rhythm.

'Alive! Alive! Alive! Alive! Alive! ALIVE! ALIVE! ALIVE!'

Today one of my friends, Tibor Hirsch, got a letter from Romania. It said that his wife was alive and at home. Yet three people have already told me they are absolutely certain they saw her being shot in Belsen.

This triumphant episode inspired Miklós to make one last attempt to win permission for his journey.

He knew that Dr Lindholm spent Wednesday evenings working in his office in the main building. So he borrowed a coat to put on over his pyjamas, walked across the yard and knocked on his door.

Dr Lindholm motioned for him to sit down while he finished his sentence, and then looked up. The room was lit by a desk lamp, and its circle of light ended just under the doctor's eyes. This put Miklós off slightly.

'I'd like to speak to you about the soul, doctor.'

Lindholm's chin and nose were in the light. 'Yes, is a strange thing.'

My father took off his coat and threw it on the floor. He was sitting there in his frayed stripy pyjamas like a mediaeval saint. 'Sometimes it's more important than the body,' he said.

Dr Lindholm clasped his hands. 'A psychologist is coming next week.'

'No, I want to discuss this with you. Have you read *The Magic Mountain*?'

Dr Lindholm leaned back, his face disappearing in the darkness. He became headless. 'Yes, I have.'

'I'm a bit like Hans Castorp. The wry envy that I feel for the healthy almost hurts … '

'Is understandable.'

'Give me permission. Please.'

'How does that fit in?'

'If I could go and see my cousin, just for a few days. If I could pretend to myself that I was cured.'

Dr Lindholm interrupted. 'Is becoming obsessive, Miklós. Drop it, for goodness sake!'

'Drop what?'

'This travel madness! This stubborn behaviour. Come to senses!' Dr Lindholm was almost shouting. He got up and stepped out of the light.

Miklós jumped up too. He also raised his voice. 'I have come to my senses. I want to travel!'

'But you will die. You will die soon!'

Dr Lindholm's terrifying diagnosis circled them like a bird of prey. Miklós could see only the doctor's two well-lit legs in their suit trousers, and decided that his verdict could therefore be ignored.

In the ensuing silence only their rapid breathing could be heard.

Dr Lindholm turned round, ashamed, and went to the cupboard. He opened the door. Shut it. Opened it again. Shut it.

Miklós stood still, growing pale.

'I'm sorry. I'm sorry. I'm sorry,' Lindholm said softly in Swedish.

He opened the cupboard again, took out a file, went over to the backlit wall and flicked the switch there. The room was flooded with cold, sterile light. The doctor removed some X-rays from the file and held them in front of the pane of glass on the wall. There were six of them. He didn't turn round. He didn't catch my father's eye.

'By the way, where is your "cousin" being treated?'

'In Eksjö.'

'Take off pyjama jacket. I listen to your chest.'

Miklós slipped out of his jacket.

Lindholm took out his stethoscope. 'Deep breathings. In, out, in, out.'

They avoided each other's eyes. Miklós breathing. Dr Lindholm listening. He listened for a long time, as if he were enjoying some distant, celestial music.

'Three days,' Dr Lindholm said. 'To say goodbye.'

Miklós pulled on his pyjama jacket. 'Thank you, doctor.'

> Lili,
>   Now you have to be quick and nimble because we're going to trick the Red Cross. I need a letter in Swedish from your doctor in which he recommends my visit on medical grounds. I've already managed to persuade my doctor!

Dr Lindholm fiddled awkwardly with his stethoscope. In the strange, intimate glow he was brave enough to take his wallet out of his back pocket. 'Finish with her. Is my opinion as a doctor, but what matters my opinion? The soul ... sometimes you have to bury it.'

He took the X-rays down from the wall and put them back in the file. He switched off the backlit wall. Now, he took a small, creased photo out of his wallet and handed it to Miklós. It showed a fair-haired little girl with a ball in her hands, gazing warily into the lens.

'Who's that?' Miklós asked.

'My daughter. Not now. She die in an accident.'

My father hardly moved. Lindholm shifted from leg to leg. The floor creaked. His voice became husky. 'Life sometimes punish us.'

Miklós stroked the face of the little girl with a finger.

'Her name is Jutta. From my first marriage. Márta related second part of story to you. Jutta is first part.'

~

This time Lili and the others had planned a longer program. Sára sang eight songs with Lili accompanying her on the piano. They included two Hungarian songs, one Schumann, two Schubert and some of the popular songs from operettas.

The soldiers, in their pyjamas, and the nurses applauded loudly. On stage, Lili and Sára gave a modest and graceful bow after each song. It was to Lili's credit that Dr Svensson came too. He sat in the middle of the front row with a little girl on his lap, and after every song he stamped his feet.

At the end of the evening he went on stage to congratulate Lili, who was standing tensely by the piano. Lili looked longingly at the little girl, who hadn't been the slightest bit fidgety, but nor had she fallen asleep. In fact, she had clearly enjoyed the concert.

'Can I hold her?'

Svensson handed the girl over to Lili, and she chuckled as Lili hugged her.

Meanwhile Sára was surrounded by soldiers. It didn't take much asking for her to sing them an encore, just like that, unaccompanied. She chose 'Crane Bird High in the Sky'. A few soldiers wept, though they didn't understand a word.

Lili caught the mood too—a kind of sorrow overwhelmed her.

~

> One evening a few days ago I went into town and
> wandered around on my own in the snowy streets.

It was dusk. Miklós was tired by the time he reached the top of the hill and he couldn't pedal any more. He got off his bike, pushed it about twenty metres, then stopped.

There were no curtains in the windows of the house; from where he stood beside the fence he could easily look in. The scene was like a nineteenth-century realist painting. The man reading, the woman sitting at her sewing machine, and lying between them in a wooden cradle a young child. He could even see that the child was playing with a doll and smiling.

> I could see into a worker's home. I feel very tired.
> Twenty-five years and so many awful things. I can't
> look back on a good and harmonious family life: I
> never had one. Perhaps that's why I long for one so
> much. I couldn't bear to see them any more, and
> hurried away.

Eight

LILI KEPT hugging Dr Svensson's little girl. The soldiers, moved by Sára's song, still surrounded her.

> *Crane bird high in the sky*
> *Is flying homewards*
> *The gypsy boy is walking on his way*
> *His staff in his hand.*

Dr Svensson touched Lili's arm. 'I've received a letter from the Avesta rehab centre. A colleague of mine wrote it, the head doctor. He's got a Hungarian wife.'

Lili blushed and stammered something. 'Yes.'

'It was about your cousin.'

'Oh, yes.'

'I'm not quite sure how to tell you. It's a disturbing letter.'

The little girl suddenly felt heavy in Lili's arms. She put her down. 'We've been planning for him to come and visit me.'

The doctor took his daughter by the hand. 'That's what it's about. I agree with the visit. I shall certainly give my permission.'

Lili shrieked, and grabbed at Dr Svensson's hand to kiss it. The doctor did all he could to pull his hand away.

Down among the audience Sára was singing, 'If I could only be with you once more, I'd lie beside you on your violet couch.'

Svensson held his arm behind his back. 'But there's something you should know.'

'I know everything.'

'You don't know about this.' Svensson waited. 'Your cousin is seriously ill.'

'Is he?' Lili felt a tiny pang in her heart.

'It's his lungs. Very serious. Irreversible. Do you understand? Irreversible.'

'I do.'

'I was in two minds whether to tell you. But since he's family I think you should know. It's not contagious.'

'I see. It's not contagious,' repeated Lili, as she stroked the little girl's hair.

Sára had finished her song and there was a hush except for the sound of Svensson's daughter humming, the effect of which was like a fading echo. Svensson put his finger to her lips, and the echo died away too.

'Take care of yourself, dear Lili. You're not well either. Far from it.'

Lili's mouth was dry; she couldn't say anything.

~

Miklós tried to conceal it, but Lindholm's diagnosis nagged at him. He didn't really believe the doctor, but for his peace of mind he felt it would be good to get a second opinion. So he asked Jakobovits, who in peacetime had worked in a hospital as a theatre assistant, to assess the X-rays. That meant breaking into Lindholm's office. Harry happily joined the mission; he was up for anything that had the tang of adventure.

The narrow corridor of the main building was lit by the yellow glow of a night light. Miklós, Jakobovits and Harry crept towards Lindholm's office like three hobgoblins.

Harry was carrying a piece of wire. He often boasted of having belonged to a gang of thieves before the war. Apparently he was an expert at picking locks.

He fiddled about in the keyhole for ages, giving Miklós time to regret the whole idea. Their escapade seemed almost laughable. But eventually Harry succeeded in opening the door and they were inside.

They went into action like a crack military unit. Miklós gestured to Harry which cabinet to open, and Harry fiddled around with his wire once again. They didn't dare turn on the light, but there was a full moon and Lindholm's room was bathed in an unearthly phosphorescent glow. The three men might have felt like heroes in a fairytale.

The cabinet lock clicked. Miklós reached in and ran his fingers over the files; he remembered that his was somewhere around the middle. He breathed out when he found it, took the X-rays and handed them to Jakobovits.

Jakobovits settled himself comfortably in Lindholm's armchair and, holding the images up to the light of the moon, began to study them.

Someone flung the door open, flicked the switch and flooded the room with the unforgiving light of three hundred-watt bulbs.

Márta stood in the doorway, her tiny bosom heaving. 'What are you gentlemen doing here?'

The gentlemen, all wearing uniform striped pyjamas beneath their makeshift coats, leapt to their feet. The X-rays slipped out of Jakobovits's hands. No one answered. The situation spoke for itself. Márta added to the pantomime by strolling over to the X-rays and picking them up one by one.

Then she turned to the honourable company. 'You may go.'

The men began to tramp out in single file.

'You stay here, Miklós,' Márta said.

The relief felt by the other two was palpable. The door

shut behind them. Miklós turned round with the most penitent expression he could summon. Márta had already taken up residence in Lindholm's armchair.

'What do you want to find out?'

'My friend Jakobovits is some kind of doctor,' Miklós stammered. 'Or used to be. I wanted him to take a look at the X-rays.'

'Didn't Erik assess them for you?'

Miklós looked down at his shoes with their sloppy laces. 'Yes.'

Márta stared at him for such a long time that he was forced to return her gaze. Then the head nurse nodded, as if she had taken note and understood. She stood up, put the X-rays back in the file and the file back in the cabinet. 'Erik does all he can for you. You are his favourite patient.'

'I always have a fever at dawn: thirty-eight point two.'

'New medicines are becoming available all over the world every week. Who knows what might happen?'

Something burst in my father. It happened so swiftly that he didn't even have time to turn away. It was as sudden as an earthquake. He collapsed to the floor and buried his face in his hands, sobbing.

Márta turned away discreetly. 'You've been through terrible things. You survived them. You survived, Miklós. Don't give up now, at the finishing post.'

Miklós couldn't speak. He wasn't crying any more—the

sound he made now was more like the whimpering of a wounded animal. He tried to form intelligible words, but it was as if his voice had abandoned him.

At last, he said, 'I'm not giving up.'

Márta looked at him in despair. He was huddled on the floor, his arms covering his head. She stepped closer to him. 'Good. So now pull yourself together.'

They gave each other some time. Miklós was quiet now, but he was hiding behind his arms and had curled himself up even smaller.

'Right,' he said when he could speak normally again.

'Look at me, Miklós.' Márta crouched down beside him.

My father peered out between his two bony elbows.

Márta adopted her cold, bossy head-nurse voice. 'Take deep breaths.'

He attempted to breathe evenly.

Márta conducted. 'One, two. One, two. Deep breaths. Slowly.'

Miklós's chest was rising and falling regularly. One, two. One, two.

'Slowly. Deep breaths.'

> My dearest little Lili,
> I'm not stupid, I know that the illness that keeps me here will gradually disappear. But I also know my fellow patients. I hear the terrible pity in their voices when they say, 'It's his lungs.'

~

It was November and an icy wind blew leaves around the Eksjö
hospital. There was an open, circular pavilion in its grounds, an
attractive building with a dark green wooden roof supported by
graceful white pillars. For Lili, forbidden to leave the grounds
during the week, this pavilion was a refuge. When she couldn't
stand the smell of the hospital any longer she escaped there. On
fine days she leaned against a column and bathed her face in the
fitful sunshine.

But now, hostile winds were blowing. In their dejection,
Lili and Sára were walking obsessively round and round the
columns in their thick woollen uniforms.

> My dear Miklós,
>   I am very cross with you! How can a serious, intel-
> ligent man of twenty-five be so foolish? Isn't it enough
> for you that I am fully aware of your illness and can
> hardly wait to meet you?

~

Late one afternoon, two men in suits and ties arrived in Avesta and
were taken straight to the Hungarian section. It turned out they
were from the Hungarian embassy. One of them held up a radio
bound with a ribbon, and the other made an announcement.

'This radio has been sent to you, on loan, by the Orion
factory in Hungary. Happy listening!'

Tibor Hirsch accepted the radio on behalf of the men. 'Thank you! News from home is more effective than any medicine.'

They put the radio on a table and my father looked for a socket. Harry switched it on. The tuning eye glistened green, and the radio crackled and hissed.

'Search for Budapest,' ordered one of the suited men.

Within half a minute they could all hear Hungarian. 'Dear listeners, it is five minutes past five. We are transmitting a message to Hungarians abroad from Sándor Millok, Minister for Repatriation. "Every Hungarian scattered around the world who is listening to this program should know that we are thinking of them and have not forgotten them. In the next few minutes I will outline to them and to our listeners at home the regulations devised to simplify the administrative requirements for our compatriots' return home."'

That evening the men sat out in the courtyard with the radio on the long wooden table. The light bulb swung eerily in the wind. The men usually spent half an hour before bed in the open air. By now they had been playing the radio for six hours without a break. They had put on sweaters and coats over their pyjamas and wrapped blankets around themselves. They sat right up close to the radio. The green tuning light winked like the eye of an elf.

They were listening to Senator Claude Pepper talking from Washington. The Hungarian presenter whispered his translation every few sentences. Then they listened to the news from Budapest. The fragments of sound whirled around in their heads like the wind sweeping down from the North Pole.

The second transport of major war criminals had arrived at Keleti railway station.

The pontoon bridge at Boráros Square had been officially opened.

The training of the first unit of policewomen had been successfully completed.

A competition testing the skill of waiters had taken place on Nagy Körút.

In the second round of the boxing team championship Mihály Kovács, boxing for Vasas, had knocked out Rozsnyó from Csepel.

~

It was Sunday. The Björkmans' dark grey car swung round in front of the hospital, and Lili, who had been waiting in the caretaker's office, climbed into the back seat.

After mass the Björkmans took Lili home to Smålandsstenar. They sat at the table for lunch, and Sven Björkman said grace. Mrs Björkman ladled out the soup, and her husband was pleased to see Lili's silver cross sparkling around her neck. Language difficulties kept the conversation brief.

'No news from home, Lili?' Björkman asked her in Swedish.

Lili didn't look up. She understood every word. She shook her head.

Björkman took pity on her. 'You know what? Tell us something about your father!'

Lili winced. How could she possibly?

Björkman misunderstood: he thought Lili was struggling
with his Swedish. Using his spoon for emphasis he hammered
out the words. 'Your papa! YOUR PA-PA! Papa! Daddy! Father!
Get it?'

Lili nodded. 'I could try to tell you in German, but I don't
speak it well enough.'

'It doesn't matter,' Björkman said. He wasn't to be put off.
'Tell us in Hungarian. We'll listen. Believe me, we'll understand.
Just tell us about him. In Hungarian. Come on! Fire away!'

The spoon was shaking in Lili's hand. The whole Björkman
family was looking at her, even the two boys. Lili wiped her
mouth on her napkin, put her spoon on the table and her hand
in her lap. She glanced down at the cross hanging from her
neck. 'My father, my dear father, has blue eyes … blue eyes that
shine,' she said in her soft Hungarian. 'He's the kindest person
in the world.'

The family listened, transfixed. Sven Björkman sat motionless, his head slightly to one side, enchanted by the music of the
unfamiliar language. What did he understand in the melody, in
the rhythm?

'My father isn't tall, but he isn't short either. He loves us
dearly. He's a salesman by occupation. A suitcase salesman.'

Every Monday at dawn Lili's father, Sándor Reich, trudged
down Hernád Street in Budapest carrying two huge Vulkan

cabin-trunks. In each one, like the layers of an onion, dozens of smaller and smaller cases and bags lay one inside the other.

This picture was so vivid that, even without shutting her eyes, Lili could see the shadow of her father creeping along the walls of the buildings in the spring sunshine.

'My father travels in the country all week. But at the weekend, on Fridays, he always comes home to us. We rented a flat to be near Keleti train station. On Monday mornings, Father sets out on foot with his wares and he walks down Hernád Street to the station. On Fridays, when he comes home, we are waiting for him.'

These words swept Lili into the past. They were sitting at the specially laid table in Hernád Street: Mother, Father and eight-year-old Lili. At the head of the table sat somebody else: an unshaven man, his scruffy coat buttoned up to hide his grimy, ragged shirt and torn trousers. Father had tried to take his coat from him, but he gave up. The stranger fingered the saltcellar with his dirty nails in embarrassment.

'On Friday evenings we always had a special supper to which Father invited a poor Jew. This was how he greeted the Sabbath. More often than not he invited a man from around the station.'

It was as if Sven Björkman understood Lili's words. A tear danced in the corner of his eye, but he remained hunched on his chair. His wife had an ecstatic smile on her face, and even the two boys were listening with wide eyes, between spoonfuls of soup.

'So every Friday evening we are a family of four.'

Lili didn't dare look down at the silver cross hanging round her neck.

In the evening, during the long drive back to Eksjö, Mrs Björkman described to Lili the complicated process of Swedish adoption. It didn't seem to bother her that Lili could not understand the subject of her excited monologue. She was simply relieved that at last she could speak out about what she and Sven had been planning for weeks.

The Björkman family was still waving goodbye to Lili long after she had disappeared behind the double wooden doors of the hospital.

> Dear Miklós,
>   Don't forget your promise to find a partner for my best friend Sára. She is older than I am. She has just turned twenty-two.

~

Crazed by nicotine deprivation, my father ran the short distance to the caretaker's office. He barged in without knocking. Frida and Harry shot apart.

'I just came for cigarettes,' Miklós said.

Frida leapt off Harry's lap and, not even doing up her blouse, went to the cupboard and took out a box. Its compartments were filled with various brands of cigarettes. She grinned, her breasts swinging all over the place. 'How many do you want?'

Miklós was ashamed, for her sake as well. He wanted four. Frida licked her fingers and picked out the cigarettes. Miklós fished out his coins. They swapped.

Harry embraced Frida from behind, kissing her neck. 'Give them to him free, darling. He's my best friend. It's thanks to him that I'm up to it again.'

Frida gave Miklós a coquettish look, shrugged and gave him back the coins.

> I'm really struggling with your request. There are sixteen of us Hungarians here, but there's not one that I'd choose for Sára. I wanted to take Harry with me to see you, for instance, but I've given up on that idea.

~

In Eksjö, the musical evenings were becoming more frequent. Dr Svensson even allowed Lili and Sára to skip half their afternoon rest. At two o'clock the girls shut themselves in the main hall and practised. The doctor had found some sheet music for them, too.

One of these albums included a selection of works by Leoncavallo. That week they performed his best known aria, 'Mattinata'. On the wings of this lofty song, Sára's soprano floated to the heights. She waved her arms about, enraptured. Lili took on this exaggerated romantic manner too, swooping down on the keys like a falcon.

It was a huge pity for them that they didn't have any suitable clothes to perform in. In fact they didn't have suitable clothes for any occasion. They took the stage in their hospital gowns, which were just long enough to cover their nightdresses.

Judit Gold sat among a row of soldiers, the only woman. She pulled herself up proudly; it felt good to be Hungarian.

> *L'aurora, di bianco vestita,*
> *Già l'uscio dischiude al gran sol.*
> *Dawn, dressed in white,*
> *Already opens the door to broad daylight.*

There must have been something in the atmosphere, because on the same evening in Avesta, hundreds of kilometres to the north, everyone was in high spirits.

Unaware of this synchronicity, the men began to sing the identical Leoncavallo aria. It was as if a celestial conductor had given a sign to his herald angels and called on his choir to sing the same song. Their rendition of 'Mattinata' in the barracks, at the suggestion of Jenö Grieger who spiced their performance with his accomplished guitar accompaniment, might have been slightly out of tune, but they gave the Italian everything they had.

For the soldiers in the Eksjö hospital the song's rousing power was irresistible. The hall was all smiles. Sára raised her arms high; Lili practically floated above the piano stool.

The men in the barracks were by now standing on beds and tables. Harry wormed himself in beside Grieger and conducted.

Ove non sei la luce manca,
Ove tu sei nasce l'amor!
There is no light where you are not,
Love is born where you are!

Miklós stood in the front row. He was flushed; the future seemed radiant. After all, 'Mattinata' was a hymn to love; he was certain that the others were celebrating *him* with this song.

~

I'm sending the wool, with our measurements. You
don't mind, do you?

Miklós had hinted to Lili on the telephone that he wasn't short of funds, courtesy of a Cuban uncle. The truth was that Uncle Henrik was my grandmother's elder brother, and his claim to fame was that in 1932 he absconded with the family jewels and emigrated to Cuba. He mustn't have felt too many pangs of conscience, because as soon as he got to Havana he sent a postcard to the family in Hungary raving about the wonders of his new homeland.

As a little boy my father often studied that black-and-white picture of the crowded Havana harbour on a rainy afternoon. He could only vaguely remember Uncle Henrik's face. He seemed to think he had a jaunty moustache and sparkling eyes, and that now and then he wore a monocle, but he couldn't swear to that.

On the Havana postcard, which for years members of

the family pointed at as proof of Uncle Henrik's unforgivable disloyalty, a three-funnelled ocean steamer was visible, as well as a number of Ford cars clustered on the dock. A few skinny stevedores loafing about gazed into the camera, so it was easy to identify them with Uncle Henrik's future. But my great-uncle had no intention of loading ships. Quite the contrary, as revealed by a more recent photograph, which he sent years later, with the obvious intention of tantalising his envious relations—a crystal-clear picture of Henrik embracing a mulatto woman with wide cheekbones and a dozen children underfoot.

In the photograph, Henrik and the woman are standing on a wooden veranda and Henrik has a cigar between his lips. On the back two lines were scribbled in his sloping hand: 'I'm fine. I've invested in a sugarcane plantation.'

When Miklós was struck by his passion for letter-writing, he immediately thought of his uncle as a potential source of cash. There was nothing to lose. He wrote to Henrik that he had managed to survive the war and was now being nursed in Sweden. He had an imaginary picture in his mind's eye. As a teenager he had often dreamed about Cuba after leafing through an album from the 1920s that he had found in his father's bookshop. In the picture he now imagined, his uncle was rocking in a hammock on the famous veranda. He had put on weight—he must have been at least 120 kilos. In my father's vision the veranda is set on a hillside overlooking the sea.

Whether or not Uncle Henrik lived like that or in even

greater style history doesn't say. He didn't write a single word in reply to Miklós's letter, but three weeks later a cheque arrived to the tune of eighty-five dollars.

This became my father's capital. On the day it arrived, he gave some of it to an old man smelling of vinegar, who palmed off four skeins of mud-coloured wool in return.

Now the owner of the world's ugliest wool, Miklós wrote a touching ad and placed it in *Világosság* to help Lili find her mother in Hungary. Another portion of Uncle Henrik's now less-than-princely sum he spent on three little chocolate cupcakes from an Avesta café and had them wrapped in a smart parcel bound with gold twine. His most serious investment was three and a half metres of material for a winter coat, which, trembling with indecision, he took a great deal of time to choose. Now he was ready for his journey.

Nine

MY FATHER travelled for a whole day. He had to change trains several times. He sat in different compartments: sometimes by the window; sometimes, for lack of space, jammed up against the door. At times he removed his bulky overcoat, folding it up and laying it across his knees. At other times his glasses misted up from the heat so he fished Lili's handkerchief out of his trouser pocket to wipe them. He took the greatest care of his parcel of cakes. He found a safe place for it in every compartment—in no way was it to be damaged.

Occasionally he fell asleep; when he was awake he looked

out of the window. The stations flashed by: Hovsta, Örebro, Hallsberg, Motala, Mjölby.

Sometime after Mjölby he slipped as he entered his compartment and fell on his face. The left lens of his glasses was smashed to smithereens.

I travelled to Stockholm so that I could buy my train ticket in person at the office for foreigners. You know what? I send you my kisses.
Miklós

There are two alcoves in the corridor. One of them is particularly secluded. We can sit all day under a huge artificial palm tree without anyone disturbing us. All right, then—I send you a kiss.
Lili

I want to tell you something the evening I arrive, just before we say goodnight for the first time. As for me, I send special kisses, heaps of them—not in that 'all right, then' mode.
Miklós

In Sára's repertoire there is another song that I'm sure you know—'The March of the Volunteers'. I'm so looking forward to seeing you! Till we meet, I send you many kisses.
Lili

I'm glad about the alcove in the corridor because I
don't like talking in full view. I'm stroking your hair
in my thoughts (will you let me?) and sending lots of
kisses.
 Miklós

This morning when I woke up my left eye was itching.
I told Sára it was a good sign. See you soon. Kisses.
 Lili

I'm arriving on the first of December at 6.17 p.m. I
send my love many times over.
 Miklós

~

On 1 December 1945 it was snowing hard in Eksjö. The platform
and tracks at the tiny station were not covered, but the entrance
was protected by a veranda.

Miklós was the only person to alight from the three-carriage
train. He didn't quite resemble Don Juan as he hobbled across
the platform. He leaned a little to the right because his shoulder
was dragged down by the weight of his suitcase, a dilapidated
number lent to him by Márta. It was tied up with string. In his
left hand he carried the cupcakes.

Lili and Sára were waiting outside the station. Lili clung
nervously to her friend's hand. Behind the girls stood a nurse
in a full-length black cloak and trademark peaked cap. She had

been instructed by Svensson to keep an eye on his patients.

Miklós spotted the reception committee in the distance and smiled. His metal teeth glimmered in the weak light of the platform lamps.

The girls glanced at each other in alarm, then looked guiltily back towards the platform where Miklós was advancing through the thick veil of snow. He had to rest for a moment while he coughed. The left lens frame of his glasses was stuffed with scrunched-up newspaper—that day's *Aftonbladet*—an operation he had performed in desperation half an hour earlier, leaving a crack free so that he could at least see a little. He drew nearer on the snow-covered platform; his borrowed winter coat, two sizes too big for him, floated around his ankles. He seemed to have tears in his visible eye, either from the cold or from excitement. Even from this distance and despite the thick lens, the girls could make that out. And he was smiling broadly, his iron teeth in full view.

Lili was scared stiff. In a matter of seconds he would be in earshot. 'He's yours! Let's swap!' she whispered to Sára out of the side of her mouth, with her teeth clenched, like someone who's had a stroke.

By now Miklós was a few steps away.

'You be Lili! I beg you!' she pleaded.

The nurse at the back of the little group was touched to see the skinny man in his funny coat reach her patients and set his battered case down in the snow.

My father had rehearsed thoroughly for this, the most

important meeting of his life. He had put together a short but striking speech—three sentences in all—that he felt would have a magical effect. In the course of his seemingly endless journey, in the stuffy compartments, he had whispered it to himself a thousand times. But now he was struck dumb with happiness. He even seemed to have forgotten his name, but that was only because he was unable to suck air into his lungs. So all he did was extend his hand.

Sára took a quick look. At least his hand was all right. Long fingers, smooth palm. She grasped it. 'I'm Lili Reich,' she said.

Miklós gave her a firm handshake. He turned to Lili. She shook his hand vigorously.

'I'm Sára Stern, Lili's friend,' she said in a bright voice.

Miklós grinned with his metal teeth. He couldn't say a word.

They stood there. Eventually, Miklós handed the parcel of cakes bound with gold twine to Lili.

The nurse stepped forward and snatched the packet out of her hands. 'We must go!' she ordered, giving Miklós a compassionate look.

So they set out. Huge flakes of snow were falling. After a slight hesitation Sára took Miklós's arm. Lili walked beside them, her eyes on the ground. For a moment it occurred to her to take my father's other arm, but she felt it was too intimate. The nurse followed, carrying the elegant parcel of cupcakes.

To get to the hospital they had to cross an enormous park. As they trudged through the virgin snow, Miklós had one arm in Sára's. In his other hand he carried the suitcase tied up with string. Lili and the nurse were a few paces behind.

In the middle of the park, precisely eight minutes after his terrifying dumbness, as if a gift from God, Miklós got his voice back. He cleared his throat, then stopped. He put down the suitcase, withdrew his arm from Sára's and turned to Lili.

It had stopped snowing. The four of them resembled figures out of a Hans Christian Andersen fairytale: dark crumbs on an oval white china plate.

Miklós abandoned the speech he had practised. 'I always imagined you like this,' he said in his pleasant baritone, 'in my dreams. Hello, Lili.'

Lili stood there awkwardly. She nodded. The weight lifted from her; everything seemed natural. She took a step forward and so did Miklós. They hugged each other.

Sára and the nurse instinctively drew back.

Half an hour later Miklós and Lili were in the alcove behind the palm. Two worn upholstered armchairs stood opposite each other. My father draped his overcoat over the back of one of them and put his suitcase down.

They sat and looked at each other, not wanting to speak. At times they smiled. They were waiting.

Miklós took the suitcase onto his lap, undid the string and opened the lid. He had packed the coat fabric on top and now he smoothed it out. He lifted it up like a baby and handed it to Lili. 'I brought this for you.'

'What is it?'

'Material for a winter coat. You just have to get it made.'

'A coat?'

'You wrote that they hadn't given you a coat. Do you like it?'

Apart from the set of clothes she was given on her arrival in Sweden, Lili had one folksy skirt, a spinach-green waistcoat and a rust-red turban-like hat—all presents from the Björkmans. As she ran her hand down the thick, dark-brown, woollen fabric it reminded her of peacetime. She held back her tears.

'I took an hour choosing it,' Miklós added. 'I'm no expert when it comes to winter coats. Or summer coats for that matter.'

Lili again fingered the material, almost as if she were trying to decipher a secret code woven into it. Then she held it to her nose. 'It's got a nice smell.'

'I brought it in that old suitcase. I was afraid it'd get creased. But it hasn't, thank God. I borrowed the suitcase from the head nurse.'

Lili remembered everything. She had read each letter from Miklós at least five times. The first time hastily devouring it, then, escaping to the bathroom, twice more, thoroughly relishing every paragraph. Later, perhaps a day later, she would reread it twice, and behind each word she imagined other words. She knew a great deal about Márta.

'Mickey Mouse?'

'Yes.'

There was so much my father wanted to tell her. The sentences piled up in his head. Where to start?

He found a cigarette in his pocket. He took it out along with a box of matches. 'Do you mind?'

'Of course not. What about your lungs?'

'They're fine. All's well here inside,' he said pointing to his chest. 'It's just my heart! It wants to burst—it's beating so hard!'

Lili stroked the coat fabric with her fingertips.

Miklós lit up. Soon a cloud of grey smoke swirled above their heads.

At last they began to speak, eagerly, hardly finishing their sentences, cutting in on each other. They were excited and impatient, wanting to make up for everything all at once. But they never spoke about certain important things. Neither then, nor later.

~

My father never told Lili that for three months he burned bodies in Belsen concentration camp.

How could he have spoken of the suffocating stench that lingered over the mounds of the dead and clawed at his throat? Is there a word that could describe this work? A phrase that could describe the feeling as bare, scaly arms slipped from their grip, over and over, to land with a senseless thud on top of other frozen bodies?

Lili did not tell Miklós about the day of her liberation from Belsen.

It took her nine hours to drag herself from the barracks to

the clothes depot, a distance of about a hundred metres. She was naked and the sun was scorching. The Germans had fled by then. All she could remember was that it was late afternoon when she made it. Then she was sitting in a German officer's tunic, leaning back against a wall and bathing her face in the light.

How did she come to be dressed in a German officer's uniform?

Miklós could never bring himself to tell her of his time, before he burned corpses, as an orderly in the typhoid barracks. In block seventeen, the most ghastly block in the camp, he doled out bread and soup to the half-dead. He had to wear the black band of the *Oberpfleger* on his arm. How could he possibly have told her about the time when Imre Bak knocked on the window? How Imre got down on all fours and barked like a rabid dog? Imre Bak was his best friend in Debrecen. He was hoping to get medicine from Miklós. Perhaps. Or at least a kind word. But he couldn't even walk into the typhoid death block. Through the filthy window, my father watched him topple over. His handsome, clever head landed in a puddle. He was dead.

And Lili never said a word—neither then nor later—about her twelve-day journey to Germany in a freight wagon. On the seventh day she discovered she could lick the condensation that had frozen overnight on the wall of the wagon. She was so thirsty, so dreadfully thirsty! Her friend Terka Koszárik had been screaming beside her nonstop for twenty hours. Perhaps Terka was the luckier of the two: she had gone completely mad.

And my father never described the murderous fight in the Belsen general hospital after the camp was liberated. He weighed twenty-nine kilos at the time. Someone had put him on the back of a truck, which took him to hospital. Afterwards, for weeks, he just lay on a bed. Three times a day a strapping German nurse picked up his featherweight body and poured cod-liver oil down his throat. Lying beside him was a dentist, a Polish Jew. He was thirty-five and spoke several languages. He could talk about Bergson, Einstein and Freud. Six weeks after liberation, this dentist beat an even more unfortunate Frenchman almost to death for half a kilo of butter. My father never spoke about that.

True, Lili never talked about the Belsen general hospital either. It was May, springtime, the war had just come to an end. She was lying there, not far from my father, as it happened, in the women's section. Lili was given paper and pencil. The task was to write down her name and date of birth. Lili thought hard. What was her name? She couldn't remember. Not for the life of her. She was devastated by the thought that she might never again remember her own name.

They didn't speak about any of these things.

Two hours later my father stroked Lili's hair, then got up awkwardly from his armchair and kissed the tip of her nose.

It was past midnight when a nurse took up position at a discreet distance, and Lili realised that it was time to say goodnight. The nurse accompanied Miklós down to the first floor and took him to a four-bed ward where he was to sleep for the next two nights.

Miklós undressed and got into his pyjamas. He was flooded with such happiness that for hours he paced the short distance from the window to the door and back again. Still exhilarated at 3.30 a.m., he had to force himself to get into bed. But he couldn't sleep.

After breakfast, at nine the next morning, they were sitting once more under the palm. When Judit Gold hurried down to the caretaker's office at 11 a.m. to bring up the mail for the women's section, she caught sight of Lili and Miklós in the alcove, their heads together, whispering. She turned away, ashamed of the spurt of breathless jealousy that took hold of her.

Lili was preparing to reveal her deepest secret. She took a breath. 'I've a terrible sin to confess. No one knows about it. Not even Sára, but I'm going to tell you.'

Miklós leaned forward and touched her hand. 'You can tell me anything. Everything.'

'I'm so ashamed ... I ... I ... ' Lili faltered.

'You've nothing to be ashamed of,' my father said confidently.

'I can't explain it ... it's awful. When we had to give our personal details, before we got on the Swedish ship ... I can't bear to tell you ... '

'Of course you can!'

'I ... I ... Instead of my mother's name—her name is Zsuzsanna Herz—instead of her name, for some reason I can't understand, I was incapable of saying her name. I lied! I just couldn't give them my mother's name.'

Lili grabbed Miklós's hand and held it tight. Her face was so pale it seemed almost luminous. My father freed himself and lit a cigarette as he always did when he wanted to think hard.

'It's quite clear: you wanted to change your fate.'

Lili thought about this. 'That's right. What a lovely way of putting it! Changing one's fate. A solution presented itself on the spur of the moment, without my really preparing for it. To be different. Not Jewish. With just one word I was transformed.'

'From a frog to a princess.'

My father always loved images from fairytales. But, perhaps because he felt this was a bit trivial, he added, 'I felt the same way. But I was too much of a coward.'

'Lying on the stretcher there on the quay, I said my mother's name was Rozália Rákosi. Where on earth did I get that name from? Rákosi? I haven't a clue. Rozália Rákosi. That's what I said instead of my mother's real name.'

Miklós stubbed out his cigarette in the tin ashtray. 'Don't worry. It's over and done with.'

Lili shook her head. 'No, it isn't. You see, I also said that my father was a Jew but my mother was Roman Catholic. Not only that, I told them I was Catholic, too. Do you see? I wanted to be done with the whole thing. The Jewish business. Once and for all.'

'Quite understandable.'

Lili started to cry.

Miklós took out his precious handkerchief.

Lili hid her face in her hands. 'No, no, it's a terrible sin! Unforgivable! You are the first person I've ever told. And, if you

want to know, every Sunday I go to a Swedish family for lunch.
The Björkmans. Everyone thinks I go there because I want to.
But that's not true, I go there because they are Catholics, too.
And I go to church with them. I've even got a cross!'

Lili pulled a creased envelope from the pocket of her gown.
She unfolded it and took out the silver cross.

Miklós turned it over in his hand. 'That makes things clear.'

'Makes what clear?'

'Why your mother hasn't been in touch yet. Why she hasn't
written to you.'

Lili took the cross, slipped it in the envelope and put it back
in her pocket. 'Why hasn't she?'

'The list! The one that appeared in so many Hungarian
newspapers. The official list. You would be on it as Lili Reich,
mother's name Rozália Rákosi. That would be a different girl,
not you. I imagine your mother read the list in Budapest and saw
your name but didn't realise it was actually you. She was looking
for a Lili Reich whose mother's name was Zsuzsanna Herz.

Lili stood up and raised her arms high, like a classical
statue. A moment later she fell down on her knees in front of
Miklós and started to kiss his hands. He stood up and hid his
arms behind his back in embarrassment. Lili stayed kneeling,
but she calmed down a little.

'This warrants a celebration!' she said in a whisper, looking
up at my father. 'What a clever man you are!'

She was already flying down the corridor. 'Sára! Sára!' she
shouted.

Ten

AT MIDDAY, in the cavernous and ugly yellow-tiled canteen where the girls ate their lunch half an hour after the men, Miklós felt that at last the hour had come for him to give an unforgettable account of his view of the world.

That winter twenty-three women were being treated on the third floor of the Eksjö hospital. They were all gathered around Miklós, including the three Hungarian girls, Lili, Sára and Judit. Using a small, sharp, wooden-handled knife Miklós sliced the three little chocolate cakes—gems of a confectioner in Avesta—into pieces. He first cut the cakes in half, then into quarters, then eighths. Soon twenty-four tiny pieces of cake were laid out in front of him, each one hardly bigger than a woman's fingernail.

Miklós stood on a chair — he was in his element. He removed his broken glasses. 'I will now explain communism to you,' he declared in an elevated form of German. 'At the core there is equality, fraternity and justice. What did you see a moment ago? Three small chocolate cakes. Three of you girls could have wolfed them down in no time. Instead, I cut up the three cakes — which, let's say, could stand for bread, milk, tractors or oil fields. I cut them into equal pieces. And, lo! Now I'll divide them among the people. Among you. Help yourselves.'

He pointed to the cakes on the table. It didn't really matter whether or not Miklós's wit had penetrated. Roused by the performance they reached for the plate, and everyone picked up a piece of cupcake. Lili looked at my father with pride.

The morsels of cake disappeared down their throats like breaths of air.

'No one has ever explained the essence of communism so beautifully,' remarked Sára, growing emotional.

Judit was the only one not to eat her now symbolic portion of cake. She turned it over in her hand until it had melted and the sticky, dark-brown goo dripped from her fingers.

~

In the early evening of 3 December, under the supervision of the cloaked nurse, Lili escorted my father to the railway station.

When the train set off, Miklós was hanging off the last step of the last carriage, and he didn't stop waving until the station had vanished.

Her eyes glistening, Lili remained on the snowy, frozen platform for a long time.

~

Miklós shut the door of the carriage behind him. He was on his way.

On the second night of his visit to Eksjö, in the four-bed ward, he had composed a love poem. On the following day, if he was on his own for a moment in the bathroom or the lift, he polished and corrected it. He hadn't dared recite it to Lili. But now, as the wheels of the train knocked against the joints in the tracks, the quickening clatter drew forth the music of his poem.

It yearned to come out of him. It wanted to burst out with such force that Miklós, even if he had wanted to, couldn't fight against it. He walked the length of the train, carrying his suitcase tied up with string. The newspaper jammed in his glasses was by this time in tatters; this didn't worry him in the slightest. He was reciting his poem. Out loud. In Hungarian.

The poem soared above the noise of the wheels. Miklós, like a cross between a troubadour and train conductor, marched the length of the carriages. He left half-empty compartments behind him without regret. He had no intention of sitting down. Instead he wanted to form some sort of bond with his fellow travellers, strangers who were staring in astonishment or sympathy at this passenger holding forth in an unfamiliar language. Maybe some of them could sense in him the lovesick minstrel. Maybe some thought he was a harmless madman. Miklós didn't give a damn; he walked on, reciting his poem.

For thirty hours of endless trails
My life has run on glowing rails
I looked in the mirror seeing how
Wonderfully happy I am now
Thirty hours—the minutes don't linger
Yet with each minute, my love grows stronger
Promise to hold on and never let go
Of my hand that you found thirty hours ago
Arm in arm each storm we'll weather
Smiling as in the alcove together.
You'll be my conscience; you'll urge me to fight
To stand up bravely for all that's right
Justice bids me to battle for all
I'm one of millions to answer the call
With ease and conviction to each task I'll rise
Helped by two stars, your beautiful eyes!

This was the poem that Miklós had been preparing for all his life. Yes, this was poetry itself. It had looped its way out from the pit of his stomach, spiced by the music of his heart and the precise mathematics of his brain. Once he had got to the end of the poem, he went back to the start. He recited it three times and the end flowed into the beginning. The Hungarian lines burning inside him flowed over the icy Swedish tracks.

Later, when he had calmed down, he settled into an empty compartment. He was convinced that the fire inside him was burning him up. Did he have a fever? Even his bones were hurting, and it was as if his skin had thinned, just as it had at dawn every day. He always kept his thermometer with him, in his pocket, in its handsome metal case. He took it out, put it in his mouth, shut his eyes and started counting. He was surprised to find that his symptoms had deceived him. The mercury stood at 36.3 — there was nothing to be alarmed about.

Miklós looked through the window. Dark snowy fields and slim pine trees flashed by.

> My dearest, dearest Lili,
>   How can I thank you for those three wonderful
> days? They have meant more to me, much more, than
> anything else ever did.

All he had to do was shut his eyes to see himself and Lili shielded by the palm in the alcove of the corridor. The two armchairs with their worn upholstery. The overcoat lying over the back of one of the chairs, the fibre suitcase on the stone floor. The awkward silence of the first half-hour as they looked at each other, not wanting to speak.

> My darling little Lili,
>   Now I'm going to tell you about the impressions
> you left in me.

First picture: the evening of the first of December.
The palm, that indiscreet tree, waving its greenery
as you smile and close your eyes. You're such a good
person and so awfully charming!

Lili had suddenly thought of a question. If my father had
had any talent for music he might even have been able to determine the tone.

'Is that today's paper?' she asked, as if she were a school-
teacher. Miklós wasn't sure what she meant. What paper?

Lili reached across and took off his glasses. She held them
up and tried to make out the words on the scrap of scrunched-up
newspaper. The awkwardness between them evaporated.

The next day: your eyes beneath your red turban as
we walk arm in arm along the street. Oh, for that little
backstreet where the cinema is!

They had walked down the Kaserngatan in a howling wind,
Miklós in the middle. Lili and Sára linked arms with him while
he tried to explain things above the noise of the gale. He talked
about his mother's special poppyseed pudding and the anthro-
pomorphism of the German philosopher Feuerbach, and he
finished up with the Swede Linnaeus's classification of plants.
At last he could put to good use all those hours spent perched on
the top rung of the ladder in the Gambrinus bookshop.

They were freezing by the time they plunged into the
cinema. The remnants of Uncle Henrik's eighty-five dollars were

nestled in Miklós's pocket. A soppy American film was playing, and my father felt the title was symbolic—*The Love Letters*. There was hardly anyone in the cinema. The three of them sat in the back row, Miklós between the two girls. He looked at the screen only for a moment or two. The *Aftonbladet* lens now proved a huge advantage: he could stare at Lili's profile, almost unnoticed, without employing any particular artifice. In a brave moment, when the dumb hero slipped on a patch of oil and slid on his bottom to the feet of his giggling love, Miklós tentatively touched Lili's hand. She squeezed his fingers in return.

> I won't write any more—it's suddenly hit me that it's
> all over. But afterwards, on the walk home, at the
> crossroads in the park, for a moment …

By the time they were in the park—at the centre of which, carved in stone, sat Carl Linnaeus himself—it was getting dark. Miklós made up his mind.

Sára tactfully walked two or three metres ahead, holding her palms out as if she were undertaking snowflake research for a meteorological institute. Miklós appreciated her tact. They walked past the gaze of Linnaeus's stone eyes. The snow was crisp beneath their boots, and the stars actually sparkled.

My father stopped Lili, stroked her face with his burning fingers—an inexplicable phenomenon in minus ten degrees without gloves—and kissed her on the lips. Lili snuggled into him and returned his kiss. Linnaeus was meditating above them.

Reassured that she could no longer hear the disappointing crunch of two pairs of feet behind her, Sára walked to the edge of the park. She began to count to herself. She was still alone when she got to 132, which gave her a good feeling. She smiled. Her heart, too, was beating hard.

> Monday. A quiet day. Only the photographer. I bet
> you, too, were wondering what your mother would say
> about our combined portrait.

The photography studio was at 38 Trädgårdsgatan. Miklós picked up the black-and-white leaflet advertising the place to save it for posterity. The photographer looked like Humphrey Bogart: a tall, handsome young man in a jacket and tie. He fiddled around with the positioning for a while, looking for the right angle. Miklós winced in jealousy every time Bogart gently touched Lili's knee to get her to move to the left or right. Then, from under the black cover behind his camera, he fussed for ages about how they should hold their heads. Eventually he emerged, rushed up to my father and started to read the news-paper stuffed into the frame of his glasses. He asked my father to take off his glasses, and then vanished under the cover again. For five or six minutes he positioned the camera at different angles. Then he came out once again, walked over to my father and whispered in his ear.

Miklós blushed. Bogart, using a very proper form of German, warned him that even if he, as the photographer, could discern that my father was aware of the problem, it didn't alter the fact that those somewhat uninviting metallic teeth were, in this powerful light, shining like mad. As a quality photographer, he felt that it was his responsibility to advise that an ideal family portrait might best be achieved if Lili were to laugh outright while my father was just beginning to form a smile. This is what he for his part would advise.

Half an hour later, the photographer of Trädgårdsgatan had finally taken my mother and father's first photo together.

> That evening you came downstairs with me, then you
> got into the lift, pulled the grating shut and, before it
> moved upwards, I leaned in once more.

The second night, Lili had made a foray down to the first floor for a goodnight kiss from Miklós. She was already in her nightdress and dressing-gown. She said goodnight to my father outside the lift, while the nurses were coming and going in the corridor. Lili got in. She pulled the iron grating across. Miklós managed to squeeze his head in between the bars, and in this hopeless position he tried to kiss her. In fact, he pressed his head towards her with such force that the white bars left their outline on his cheeks. The lift went up. Miklós couldn't bring himself to leave. He was still waiting for Lili's slippers to disappear when he felt a hand on his shoulder.

Dr Svensson was standing beside him in his white coat. 'You speak German, don't you?'

'I speak it and understand it.'

'Good. I'd like to call your attention to something.'

Miklós had no doubt what the doctor was referring to. But right now, at this rather special moment, he had no wish to launch into a discussion about the state of his health. 'I'm aware of everything, doctor. Currently my lungs are—'

'I wasn't thinking of you,' Svensson interrupted. 'You misunderstand me.'

Miklós breathed out.

'All I wanted was to ask you to take good care of Lili,' Svensson continued. 'She is no ordinary girl.' Dr Svensson took Miklós by the arm and guided him down the corridor. There was no one else around.

'You see, by a cruel stroke of fate, I happened to be on the international team of doctors present when the women's camp in Belsen was liberated. I'd like to forget that day. But it's impossible. We thought we'd found everyone who showed the tiniest sign of life. Only the dead remained, lying on the bare concrete … nearly three hundred childlike bodies, naked, or in rags. Skeletons weighing twenty kilos.'

Svensson stopped for a moment in the deserted hallway and stared into the distance. He seemed agitated. Miklós looked at him in surprise; the doctor's face was distorted into a strange grimace, as if he were in pain.

'We were on our way out. I looked back once more, just in case … I couldn't decide whether I was seeing things or … if a finger really did move. Do you understand, Miklós? Look … like the last flutter of a dove's wing … or the ripple of a leaf once the wind has died down.' Svensson raised his hand and crooked his index finger. His voice cracked. 'And so we brought Lili back among us.'

~

Years later, it always sent a chill down my father's spine when he recalled Svensson's expression and his hand held up with its quivering finger. And all this merged inseparably with another memory from his visit to Eksjö.

When the train puffed away and he was standing on the last step of the last carriage and waving until the station had disappeared, he was overjoyed that he could summon up Lili's true image. All he had to do was shut his eyes—his last glimpse of her was etched forever into his memory. Lili was waving on the snowy platform. She was crying. And her fingers—my father claimed that he had watched her delicate hand and those slender fingers almost as though they were in close-up on a cinema screen. This, of course, was impossible at such a distance, especially with his smashed glasses, but even so. He was clinging to the open carriage, the train was gaining speed and he, behind his closed eyelids, really did see Lili's fingers as they trembled in the wind like leaves.

~

'Take care of her. Love her,' Svensson instructed Miklós on that last evening in the hospital. 'It would be so good if ... '

He fell silent for so long that Miklós wondered if he was searching for the appropriate word in German. 'What would be so good?' he asked.

Svensson still didn't speak. All at once it clicked—Svensson wasn't having trouble with his German. He had arrived at a boundary that he didn't want to cross. He never finished his sentence, but he gave Miklós a hug, which said more than any words could.

~

In Ervalla, Miklós changed trains. He found a window seat. In the foreground of the night landscape, his own tired, stubbly face was reflected in the glass.

> On Tuesday I got up in a bad mood: it was the last
> day. We walked again to Stadshotell Square like we
> had on Sunday evening. And I could only steal one or
> two furtive kisses from you on the way.

That last evening, they sat again in the two armchairs behind the palm. Lili was crying. Miklós held her hand; he couldn't think of anything encouraging to say.

'I dreamed about our flat last night,' Lili said. 'I saw Papa getting his suitcases ready. It was a Monday and just beginning to get light. I knew he would be setting off soon. In my dream I knew we wouldn't see him for a week. Isn't that odd?'

She forgot about crying and that she was in hospital in a foreign country. She talked as if she were recalling the previous day's picnic. When she was a child, her father's routine had seemed like a jigsaw puzzle. Sándor Reich, suitcase salesman, prepared his wares at dawn on Monday. He packed two medium-sized suitcases into two trunks, and the smaller cases into the medium-sized ones. And he crammed the briefcases and handbags into a red children's suitcase. It was quite incredible that all those leather goods could fit into two trunks.

The truth was that Lili's strong attachment to her parents disturbed Miklós. He had only one clear memory of his father. He couldn't quite decide whether the scene remained so vivid because he saw it once or because he saw it many times. Maybe every Sunday lunch had ended in this way.

My grandfather always tucked his damask napkin into the collar of his shirt. His thick hair shone with brilliantine. My grandmother, who always looked rather dishevelled, was taking a spoonful of soup. Pea soup, yes. A white china tureen of yellowy-green pea soup with globules of fat floating on the surface sat in the middle of the table. Beside it was a small dish piled with croutons. Miklós remembered every detail. He was just a boy, sitting opposite his mother in a black waistcoat. His father started shouting; he tore the napkin from his neck, jumped up and with a single movement yanked off the tablecloth.

My father never forgot it. The pea soup shot out of the tureen. The yellowy-green liquid flowed onto his knees, burning him, and the croutons dropped to the floor like tiny winged angels.

He told Lili this story, holding her hand, that evening under the palm.

Lili changed the subject. 'I don't want to be … '

'What don't you want to be?'

'It's so dreadful to say it. But I want to be different.'

'Different?'

'Different from Mama and Papa.'

Judit Gold appeared, carrying cups of tea. She couldn't help overhearing. 'What don't you want to be, Lili?'

Lili looked from her to Miklós. 'I don't want to be Jewish!' she replied in a quiet, resolute tone.

There might have been a hostile edge to her words.

'It's not a question of wanting or not wanting,' retorted Judit, wiping a drop of tea off the table with her finger. She marched off as if Lili had personally offended her.

Miklós was pensive. 'I know a bishop. We'll write to him. We'll apply for a conversion. All right?'

As usual, my father had exaggerated things a bit. He wasn't acquainted with any kind of bishop. But he was convinced that sooner or later, if he looked, he'd find one.

'You don't mind?' asked Lili, stroking my father's hand.

'It had occurred to me, too,' said my father equitably.

~

On the night train back to Avesta, as the stations flashed past, Miklós thought through the problem. For him the question of conversion was irrelevant. It didn't mean a thing to him that he was Jewish. As a teenager, he was so hooked on the new socialist ideology that there was no room left for anything antiquated. If conversion was important for Lili, if that was what she wanted, then he would get hold of a priest. Or a bishop. Or the pope himself, if it came to that.

He had gone through Örebro, Hallsberg, Lerbäck and Motala. Miklós was writing a letter.

> You can see, can't you, dearest Lili, what a devoted soldier I am in the cause of freedom and the oppressed, the cause that has awakened the sons and daughters of every nation. You'll be my companion in everyday life (you will, won't you?), so be my faithful companion in this, too! You were once a bourgeois girl—now you should become a tough and militant socialist! You do feel so inclined, don't you?
>
> I'll contact the bishop as soon as I get back to Avesta. I'm counting the days until Christmas when I hope I'll see you again!
>
> Many, many hugs and kisses,
> Miklós

Eleven

THE DAY after Miklós left Eksjö, at the end of the communal breakfast, Dr Svensson came in and tapped a spoon against a glass. The hum of chatter died away.

Svensson seemed nervous. 'I would like you all to remain patient and trusting. I have just received news that will bring certain changes to your lives. The Swedish Ministry of Health has decided to disband the Smålandsstenar rehabilitation hospital with immediate effect. This means that patients who have been cured in our hospital here in Eksjö will be permitted to leave. Others will be moving to another facility at Berga.'

Svensson wanted to say more, but no one could hear him

in the eruption of joy. The girls stood up on their chairs, some of them hugging each other, even screaming. Others tried to get close to Svensson, speaking to him in various languages. He tapped his glass to take control of the situation, but it was hopeless.

> This morning, in the midst of bedlam, they
> announced that the hospital here will be shut down,
> and we are moving to a vast rehab centre several
> hundred kilometres away—very soon. And it is my
> turn to visit you. But at least I'll be a bit nearer to you
> and won't have so far to travel when I come.

The three Hungarian girls went straight to their ward. They were about to start packing when Lili noticed the theft.

Half an hour later, a committee was trying to get the facts of the case, but Lili was in no condition to answer questions. She had one fit of crying after another, and finally she was given a sedative. She lay curled up on her side on her bed and didn't say a word.

So for the hundredth time Sára had to tell those concerned what had happened. 'I said that before. It was open,' she reported, pointing to the only cupboard, in the corner of the room.

The cupboard, which the girls had used to store their things, was still wide open and more or less empty.

A bespectacled man was whispering a translation of Sára's words into Swedish for the benefit of the local head of the Red Cross, a tall blond scowling fellow with amazingly pale skin.

Madame Ann-Marie Arvidsson was also there, writing the report. 'What did the material look like?' she asked.

Sára stroked Lili's curled back. 'What was it like, Lili? I only saw it once.'

But Lili just stared at the birch tree swaying in the breeze.

Sára did her best. 'It was brown fabric fit for a winter coat. Tweed, with a nap. She got it from her cousin.'

The man in glasses translated in a whisper. 'It must have happened while we were hearing the news in the dining hall. Everyone was downstairs.'

Ann-Marie Arvidsson put down her pen. 'There's never been a theft in this hospital before. I really don't know what to do,' she said.

'I do!' announced the stern, blond man from the Red Cross, striking the table. 'We'll find it and return it to the owner.'

~

When my father arrived back in Avesta he reported to the office, then walked across to the barracks to change. It was midday; everyone would be in the canteen.

Miklós caught sight of him immediately and backed away. The booted feet formed an arc above the middle row of beds. The suitcase slipped out of Miklós's hand. He took off his glasses and wiped the good lens. When he put his glasses back on, it was clear that he hadn't imagined it. From where he was standing one of the metal cupboards blocked his view of the upper part of the barracks. But when he moved forward he saw the torso too: the grey trousers and the belt around the waist.

It was Tibor Hirsch. He had hung himself. From a hook—a thick, bent nail near the overhead light. A letter lay on the ground beneath his body. Miklós's legs and hands began to tremble, he had to sit down. Minutes passed. He had an irresistible urge to read the letter. He had to overcome this trembling, this feeling of revulsion. He could see that the letter had an official stamp at the bottom. He knew what it would say even before he forced himself to stand up and shuffle over to the hanging body.

He was right, of course. He didn't need to pick it up; he could tell that the last letter in the life of the electronic radio technician and photographer's aide was a death notice. The death certificate of Mrs Tibor Hirsch, née Irma Klein.

It flashed through Miklós's mind that he had written to Lili about reports that Hirsch's wife had been shot in Belsen. That was when the triumphant conga line had taken over the barracks. What had made him suppress his misgivings? Why had he not hurried over to Hirsch and shaken him to wake him up to the truth? But when? When would he have had the chance?

Was it when Hirsch sat up in bed, waving the letter above his head? Or when he yelled out, 'She's alive! My wife's alive!'? Should he have rushed over and shaken him, shouting, 'No, she isn't alive, she's dead—three people saw her shot down like a rabid dog'?

Or could it have waited? Until when? When Hirsch set out between the beds holding up the message like a flag, turning the single word into a proclamation? Then? Or when Harry joined him, grasping his shoulders from behind, and together they began to chant their marching song?

What could he have done when their fears were transformed into a glorious eruption of words? Alive, alive, alive, alive, alive! How could he have stopped this volcano?

Should he have got up on the table and shouted above the chorus? What would he have shouted? *Come to your senses! Come to your senses, you idiots. You are alone now, they've died, they've gone. All those you loved have turned into smoke. I saw it happen. I know. She's not alive, not alive, not alive, not alive, not alive!*

But instead he had joined the line and become part of the snake, a part of the whole creature that wanted to abandon its common sense, to believe that nothing had changed.

And now, here was Hirsch's lifeless body hanging from the hook.

~

That evening, when the effect of the sedative had worn off, Lili walked down to the office with Sára and made a formal complaint. Two days later, when she got a letter from Miklós— who, within a couple of hours of learning of the theft, had found out what the usual Swedish procedures were in such a case—the investigation was already underway. But both of them knew very well that Lili wouldn't be wearing a decent overcoat that winter.

My one and only darling Lili!

You must report the theft to the police saying that the culprit is unknown. You must write a letter in German in triplicate (one copy for the hospital, one for the foreigners' office and one for the police) giving exact details of the loss—three and a half metres of brown material for a winter coat, etc.

More important things were taking place. On Tuesday morning, nine girls who were convalescing at the Eksjö hospital, including the three Hungarians, were transported by bus to Smålandsstenar railway station. It was chaos at the station, and all the while it snowed.

Most of the Smålandsstenar patients were already on the train. The arrivals from Eksjö hurried along the muddy platform carrying bundles and suitcases. Dr Svensson and the nurses in their black cloaks rushed up and down beside the train, like a benevolent military brigade, trying to calm everyone down. There was an abundance of tears, kisses and mud, all accompanied by rousing music played through a loudspeaker.

Lili, Sára and Judit Gold managed to find the carriage where their friends from Smålandsstenar, whom they hadn't seen for three months, were sitting. Screams of joy and much hugging followed. Then they pulled down the windows, leaned out and blew kisses to Dr Svensson. A nurse arrived on a bicycle with a bulky leather bag on her shoulder containing that day's post—a nice touch of organisation. She had tucked her cloak up above her knees so it wouldn't get caught in the spokes. People jumped aside when she rang her bell.

'Post! Post!' she called, getting off the bike in the middle of the platform, and letting it crash to the ground. She took a batch of envelopes from the bag and read out the names. She had to shout to be heard above the music.

'Scwarz, Vári, Benedek, Reich, Tormos, Lehmann, Szabó, Beck ... '

Madame Ann-Marie Arvidsson, who was also fussing about on the platform and had a slight feeling of remorse about her treatment of Lili, pricked up her ears at 'Reich'. She took the envelope from the nurse and set out to find Lili in the crowd. She ran along beside the train, thinking it must be a letter from Miklós. She was calling Lili's name, but her chirpy voice was lost in the cacophony. Her coat was muddy up to the knees. Flushed and breathless, she held the letter above her head and shouted 'Reich, Reich'.

Then she spotted Lili hanging out of the window of a compartment a few metres away.

Lili saw her, too. 'Ann-Marie! Ann-Marie!' she yelled.

Madame Arvidsson was touched that Lili had called her by her first name. She held out the envelope and caught Lili's hand, giving it a squeeze.

'I expect it's your friend!' she said with a laugh, showing that she was on love's side.

But Lili glanced at the letter and blanched. The envelope

had a Hungarian stamp and the address was written in a spidery hand. There was no mistaking it. Lili fell backwards into the compartment. Sára had to catch her to stop her falling to the floor.

'It's Mama's writing,' she whispered, clutching the letter and pressing it to her.

'It'll get terribly creased, let go!' demanded Sára, trying to prise the envelope from her hand. But Lili wouldn't let go.

Judit stuck her head out of the window and shouted to Svensson, who happened to be going past the carriage, 'Reich's got a letter from her mother!'

Dr Svensson stopped, along with his escort. The cloaked nurses surrounded him like a flock of crows, and they all clambered aboard.

There must have been at least fifteen people crammed into the tiny compartment. Lili still hadn't dared open the letter; she kept kissing and stroking it.

'Go on, open it, Lili!' urged Svensson.

'I don't dare,' she sobbed. She handed the letter to Sára. 'You open it.'

Sára didn't hesitate. She tore the envelope open and took out several densely filled pages, which she tried to give to Lili.

But Lili shook her head. 'You read it. Please!'

Svensson, who was now sitting next to Lili, held her hand between both of his. Somehow, news had got round about the letter from Budapest. More people had gathered in the corridor and on the platform. If Sára wanted to live up to the occasion she'd have to declaim the letter as if this were a theatre performance. She was aware of the singularity of the moment, but her voice let her down. She, who could easily get through Schumann's most difficult aria, now began to read in a scratchy, faltering tone.

"'My darling, one and only Lili! I saw your notice in *Világosság* under the headline, Three Hungarian Girls in Sweden Are Looking for Their Relatives.'"

Lili could see their building with its long balconies in Hernád Street, their dark-green front door and Mama's shabby dressing-gown. The bell rings. Mama opens the door wide. Her neighbour Bözsi is there, waving that day's *Világosság* above her head and shouting. Lili wasn't sure what she was shouting, but it didn't matter. There was no doubt, though, about the shouting—the muscles in her neck were tensed, and she was tapping the newspaper on the last page where the framed notice had been set in bold letters. Mama snatched the newspaper out of her hands, took a quick look at the notice, saw the name, her name, and fainted.

Lili distinctly heard what she said either before her collapse or after she came round. 'I always knew our little Lili was a clever girl!'

After her initial nervousness, Sára got her voice back.

"'Your miraculous news arrived after a dreadful year! I can't possibly describe to you what it means to me. I can only thank the Lord that I lived to see this day.'"

Svensson was still holding Lili's hand.

Bözsi dashed into the larder muttering to herself. 'Vinegar, vinegar, vinegar.'

She found it on the second shelf, drew the cork out with her teeth and sniffed it. Then she rushed back to Mama, who was still lying in the doorway, and splashed some vinegar on her face. Whereupon Mama sneezed and opened her eyes. She looked at Bözsi, but she was whispering to Lili.

"'I'm afraid your dear, good papa isn't home yet. After he was freed he was taken to hospital in Wels in Austria with enteritis. Since May I've heard nothing. I hope that with God's help he will come home soon so that we can live our lives together in happiness again.'"

Lili wasn't sure which bits Sára was reading, and which bits she was hearing in her mother's own voice, as if Mama was sitting in the stuffy compartment and taking over at the most important parts.

"'Since 8 June, when the husband of our dear cousin Relli came home from Auschwitz, I've been living with them, and I'll stay here until one of you returns. God willing, I hope it won't be too long now!'"

The penetrating smell of vinegar filled the flat. Mama wiped her face and got to her feet with Bözsi's help, then staggered over to the kitchen tap and washed her face. After that she sat on a stool, spread the newspaper on her knees and read the notice seven times running, until she was sure she'd remember its words as long as she lived.

"'I don't even know where to begin. What do you do all day? What do you get to eat? What do you look like? Are you very thin? Have you got enough underwear? I'm afraid we were robbed of everything. We got back nothing of what we sent to the country—no bed linen, no material, no winter coat, no clothes, nothing. But don't you worry about that, my girl.'"

Lili heard that last torrent of words in her mother's voice. Mama said 'my girl' in such an unmistakable way. My girl, my girl, my girl. God Almighty, how good that sounded!

Svensson didn't understand a syllable of the letter, but his face shone with as much happiness and pride as the faces of all the Hungarian girls in the compartment. Sára looked around, swallowed and went on reading.

"'Now for some good news. The new piano that you got from your dear father on your eighteenth birthday is safe and sound! I know you'll be very pleased about that, Lili.'"

Mama sat on the stool. She smoothed out the copy of *Világosság*, already composing the letter, smiling to herself. She started writing it down straightaway. In fact she had composed it in her head every night for the past ten months, so it was no effort now to put it on paper. She knew every comma and had checked the spelling over and over—she wasn't going to make mistakes in such an important document. She muttered and hummed while she wrote.

"'If you get the chance, my darling, use a sunray lamp on your hands and feet, even your head, because I suspect some of your beautiful wavy hair might have fallen out from lack of vitamins. You might even have had typhoid. So don't forget about that, sweetheart. When, with God's help, you come home, I want you to be just as radiant as you were before.'"

Someone, probably one of the nurses from Svensson's team, rushed over to the stationmaster warning him not to let the train depart while the doctor was still aboard. Svensson himself didn't move. He was squeezing Lili's hand. The girls' bodies were pressed against each other in the compartment, their eyes shining. Sára's voice floated out through the open window onto the platform.

"'We've had no news of poor Gyúri, but all four of the Kárpátis are fine. Bandi Horn is apparently a prisoner of war in Russia. Zsuzsi isn't mentioned in your notice. What do you know about her, darling girl? You all set out together, after all.'"

The lump in Lili's throat began to swell. She and her cousin Zsuzsi were lying in each other's arms on the floor of the putrid barracks when Zsuzsi passed away—on butterfly wings, with a smile on her lips and a body scarred by millions of lice. When did she actually die? Lili would never speak to anyone about that.

In her kitchen smelling of vinegar, Mama seemed to sense that she had touched a raw patch. She became quiet: a drop of water fell from the tap. She looked at Bözsi and sobbed. Bözsi hugged her, and they cried together.

Lili could hear clearly what Mama said through her tears and with her head buried in Bözsi's neck.

"'If only I could hug you both. I've no other wish in life, but to live for that day. I'm longing for you and send you a million kisses, your adoring mama.""

Lili was almost in a trance. She didn't notice Svensson and the nurses leave. Apparently they all hugged her and kissed her before they climbed down from the train. Later, Dr Svensson and his flock stood in the snow like statues on Eksjö platform until the train disappeared.

> My one and only darling Lili!
>
> I can't tell you how utterly happy your news made me! I told you so, didn't I? I knew you'd get a letter from your mother this week. I love you more and more every minute. You're such a sweet girl, and so good. And I'm such an uncouth boy. You'll make me better, won't you?

Twelve

TWO DAYS later, Miklós disappeared. No one noticed his absence until midday. The first to miss him were Harry and Frida, who were used to him slinking into the caretaker's office before lunch to buy his two cigarettes for the afternoon. When he didn't turn up, Harry asked Jakobovits when and where he'd last seen him.

By one o'clock, Dr Lindholm, too, had been informed that his favourite patient had evaporated like camphor. They counted the bicycles, but none was missing. When Miklós didn't show up for lunch, they started to worry.

Dr Lindholm despatched a car to town in case Miklós had

gone to the post office and been taken ill on the road. In the meantime he phoned all the possible places Miklós could have been—the post office, the café, the railway station. No one had seen him. In the late afternoon he notified the police and ordered a curfew.

Everyone linked Miklós's disappearance to Tibor Hirsch's suicide. Miklós had discovered the body, and he was there when they cut Hirsch down from the rope. In the days following he had sat silently on his bed. No one could cheer him up. Later, Harry suggested that he might have wandered off to escape Christmas, which was approaching fast. There was much talk about the festivities, though many of the patients, being Jews, had never observed Christmas. On the other hand, Jenö Grieger claimed Miklós was a socialist and couldn't care less about Christmas—there was no way a man like him would be undone by a religious holiday.

Márta came into the barracks and questioned everyone individually. She spent a long time in Miklós's corner, trying to decide whether she should sift through his correspondence. He kept all his letters in a cardboard box. There were about three hundred envelopes in it, in perfect order, including Lili's letters, which were bound separately with a yellow ribbon. Márta picked up the box, then resisted the temptation. She decided it was too soon. She would give him until the next morning.

At that moment, my father was wandering in the pine forest, lost in thought, seven kilometres away. He couldn't explain to himself why feelings of anxiety and depression had overwhelmed him that morning. It was no different from any other morning. He took his temperature at dawn, and then had breakfast. He wrote a letter to Lili. He played a game of chess with Litzman and then walked to Dr Lindholm's office for a quick check-up and to pester him about Lili visiting at Christmas.

Maybe that was it. The offhand glance with which Lindholm sent him on his way. The doctor listened to his lungs and shrugged. Shrugged!

Miklós stopped in the forest. There was a gentle breeze. Yes, it was Dr Lindholm's thoughtless response, like the first domino falling, that had set the whole thing off. He had come out of the doctor's office with a sinking heart. He had never believed in this stupid diagnosis. He'd always brushed it off as a mistake. Let the clever guys talk—he knew better!

But that morning, Lindholm's casual gesture had been like a blow to the stomach. It took his breath away. He was going to die! He was going to disappear like Tibor Hirsch. His cupboard would be emptied, his bed stripped. And that would be it.

So he left. He trudged through the gate and walked to the crossroads where, instead of turning left to go to town, he turned right towards the forest. He'd hardly ever walked that way before. The paved road soon gave way to a track, which narrowed into a path that had probably been made by deer. After a while it widened out into a large snow-covered meadow. By this time Miklós was completely lost. Not that it worried him. It felt good to walk, and he rather enjoyed keeping company with death. The Grim Reaper. So what if he was going to snuff it? He had lived and loved, and this was it. He'd fade away like the deer tracks. He repeated poems to himself, silently at first, then aloud and then at the top of his voice. He walked on between pine trees that reached towards the sky, reciting poetry the whole way—Attila József, Baudelaire, Heine.

By late afternoon, after a coughing attack, he began to feel sorry for himself. He was cold, his boots were wet through, and he was so tired that he had to sit down on a fallen tree trunk. He might have been reconciled to his fate, but he had no desire to freeze to death. So he set out north, imagining the barracks was in that direction, but not at all sure he was right.

~

At eight in the evening Lindholm phoned his colleague Svensson in Eksjö. He didn't know that the Smålandsstenar patients had been moved to Berga two days earlier. Svensson was surprised to hear of Miklós's disappearance; he couldn't imagine the reason for it but he, of course, gave Dr Lindholm the telephone number at Berga. Lindholm waited until 11 p.m. to call the Hungarian girl, who probably knew more about Miklós than anyone else. For some reason he phoned from the caretaker's office, perhaps because it allowed him to keep an eye on the road, down which he hoped Miklós would come any minute.

~

It was the girls' second day in the Berga rehab hospital. They were housed in a long, stark barracks like the one at Avesta. They were already in bed when a messenger came to summon Lili to the telephone in the main building. Lili got up, found a spare coat, and set out. Sára called after her. She had her misgivings, so she put on her boots and followed.

At the exact moment that Lindholm heard Lili's thin voice issue a hesitant 'hello', he caught sight of Miklós dragging himself towards the gate.

'Is that you, Lili? I have Miklós here on the line for you,' he yelled into the phone, though he reckoned it would take my father at least five minutes to shuffle up to the caretaker's lodge. 'Hold on. He'll be here in a moment.'

~

My father didn't think he would ever get back. He was trying to retrace his steps but it felt like he was going in circles. The imprint of his boots in the snow had faded; then his footprints seemed to double up. For a terrifying period he could have sworn he was following the tracks of a bear, but then he somehow found his own boot prints again.

He was completely flummoxed when the tracks he was following came to an end in the middle of the path. They were there one moment and gone the next, as if the track-maker had taken flight.

The sun had set and it was unbearably cold. Miklós was

suffering. His feet were blistered; his head throbbed. He kept coughing. The thin sickle of a moon barely lit the forest. He often fell, sinking to his knees in the powdery snow. He lost all hope. But he knew he mustn't stop. Gathering up his remaining strength, he concentrated on nothing but walking—one-two, one-two, one-two. But it felt hopeless. He could hear the call of an animal—a hoot, he imagined—but were there owls in Sweden in winter? 'The owl screeched death'—that was a good line, a good first line, but when would he get it down on paper? Never. Never more.

And then Miklós saw the caretaker's lodge, the fence and, behind the bars on the window, Lindholm holding the telephone. Perhaps he was dreaming.

It took him a good ten minutes to make the last fifty metres. He stumbled into the lodge. Lindholm looked at him and pressed the receiver into his hand. 'Lili Reich. You want talk to her, no, Miklós?'

Lili had no idea what to make of the long delay. Since the unknown man from Avesta kept reassuring her that he was about to connect Miklós, she assumed there must be some problem with the line. The receiver hissed and crackled in her ear.

After an eternity, she heard my father's faint voice: 'Yes?'

'Are you all right?'

'Fine. Great.' What could he say?

Lili was relieved. 'We've made a little corner for ourselves in the new place at Berga.'

'And?'

'You can't imagine. It's ghastly! I don't even want to write to you about it. Do you mind me complaining?'

Miklós's facial muscles were frozen. He had no breath. He could hardly form the words. 'Don't worry.'

He was playing for time. He tried to massage his face with stiff fingers. Dr Lindholm was suffocating him too, standing so close that Miklós had to hunch over in order not to touch him.

'What's it like? Tell me,' he asked.

'Wooden barracks, bumpy paths, awful … I can't sleep at night, it is so cold. I wake up with a sore throat and a temperature.'

'I see.'

'There isn't even anywhere in the barracks where we can sit. No chairs, no table! All day we just wander around the place like stray dogs.'

'I see.'

My father went blank. He felt empty. All he wanted to do was lie down and close his eyes.

Lili realised that Miklós wasn't himself. Most of the time she could hardly get a word in. Now there was a heavy silence. 'I've been in a bad mood and terribly uptight the whole day,' she tried again. 'All I want to do is cry. I don't know where I should be. I'm so homesick.'

'I see.'

That didn't sound like Miklós's voice. The tone was icy. Almost hostile. They both fell silent.

Yesterday's call — it was dreadful. I couldn't speak
properly. I wanted to say how I love you beyond
measure and feel for you. Forgive me if I didn't say
that. Only a few days now and I'll be seeing you!

'Well, then,' Lili whispered.

'I see. I see.'

'Are you all right?'

'Yeah.'

Lili turned pale. 'I'd like you to write to my mother an
airmail letter, now that we've got her address, and tell her everything about us,' she mumbled.

Lindholm could see that all my father wanted to do was sleep.

'Right. I'll do that.'

Silence.

Yesterday when I put down the receiver I was
overcome with a strange sensation … it was as if
someone had thrown cold water on me! Your voice
sounded so alien and icy that I couldn't help feeling
that perhaps you don't love me any more.

Click. The line was cut. Lili was white as a sheet. Sára put
her arm round her.

'His voice was so different. Something has happened.'

'His friend who committed suicide,' Sára said. 'That's what's
behind it. He's got so much on his mind, poor thing.'

They walked back to the barracks arm in arm. Lili didn't
sleep at all that night.

Thirteen

A DANCE was scheduled for the next day at Berga to celebrate the arrival of the new patients. A band was to play in the cavernous hall, which they jokingly called the snack bar. A three-piece playing Swedish tunes: a pianist, a drummer and a guy on the saxophone.

Some girls danced. It didn't seem to bother them that the musicians were the only men in the hall. Most of them, though, stared into space at the wooden tables that had been specially laid out for the occasion. Beer, scones and sausage were on offer.

Lili, Sára and Judit were sitting at a table on their own when two men came into the dining room and, after making enquiries, headed straight for them.

'Are you Lili Reich?' one asked in Swedish, taking off his hat.

Lili remained seated. 'Yes, that's me,' she replied in German.

The man pulled a thin strip of fabric out of his pocket. 'Do you recognise this?' he asked, switching to German.

Lili stood up and took the piece of material from him. 'Yes, I do!' She ran her hand over it, feeling the nap with her fingertips. 'Look,' she said, handing it to Sára, 'it's my coat material, isn't it?'

The other man took off his hat. 'Let me introduce myself, ladies. My name is Svynka, I'm the district representative from Eksjö. And this is the hospital caretaker, Mr Berg.'

Mr Berg nodded, and took over. 'During the investigation at the Eksjö hospital, we found three and a half metres of the cloth that you reported missing at the bottom of a cabinet in one of the corridors. Do you follow me, Miss?'

'Yes.'

'Good. The cloth had been cut into strips.'

He asked for the piece of fabric and held it up. Lili was stunned. The band was playing a slow number, and several girls were swaying around each other on the parquet floor.

Lili wanted to make sure she had understood. She turned to Sára. 'Did I hear right? It was cut into strips?'

Sára nodded, mystified.

'It seems the thief wasn't intending to keep the material, just to destroy it,' Svynka added.

The music had changed. A lively polka started up. Only

a few girls were left on the floor, but they danced with gusto. Lili stared at the single strip of cloth dangling from the burly caretaker's fingers.

'It will be difficult to find the culprit at this stage. But, if you wish' — Berg made a sweeping gesture towards the other tables — 'we'll question everyone.'

'It won't be easy, but if that's what you want,' Svynka continued.

Lili shook her head. She couldn't speak or take her eyes off the remnant of the never-to-be winter coat between the care-taker's thumb and index finger.

Without a word, the three girls tramped the paths between the barracks in the dark, their hands in the pockets of their quilted uniform jackets. It was freezing and the wind howled.

Lili stopped. 'Who can hate me that much?'

'Someone who envies you your luck,' said Sára, with a sympathetic smile.

Judit was angry. 'I wouldn't let it go if I were you. Make them investigate to find out which girl did it. I'd like to look her in the eye!'

'How could they find out?' asked Sára.

'How should I know? Question all the girls. Search their belongings.'

'Should they look for a pair of scissors? Or a knife?' asked Lili wryly.

Judit was adamant. 'Who knows? Scissors, knife, something! Maybe a scrap of tweed!'

They walked on.

'Of course, the girl would have it on her! Next to her heart!' said Sára. 'Really, Judit, you're incredibly naïve.'

'All I'm saying is that this kind of thing should be sorted out. It shouldn't be left to fade away. That's my opinion.'

Lili was looking at the muddy, icy path. 'I have no wish to know. What would I say to her?'

'What it calls for. You'd spit on her,' Judit hissed.

'Me? Come off it! I'd feel sorry for her,' claimed Lili, even if she wasn't sure she would be so kind-hearted.

~

Dr Lindholm didn't ask Miklós where he'd gone on that desperately long day, or why. He prescribed a hot bath and something to bring his temperature down. Three days later, however, he felt it his duty to inform him, in person, of his final decision. They were sitting on the couch like old friends.

'I know this will be upsetting you, Miklós,' the doctor said, 'but I am forbidding your cousin to visit you at Christmas.'

'Why?'

'Is no room for her. Everywhere is full. But this only one reason.'

'And the other?'

'Last time I tell you, say goodbye to her, remember? But even if you were healthy, and you are not, I don't allow female visitor to male hospital. As a reading man you must understand that.'

'What should I understand?'

'You once mentioned *The Magic Mountain*? Sensuality is … how I put it … unsettling. Is dangerous.'

Miklós stood up and went to the door. Dr Lindholm's decision seemed irrevocable. What had changed in the last few days? How could Miklós have lost the doctor's sympathy? He urgently needed to do something different, something that would break Lindholm's resolve.

Gripping the doorhandle, he turned back. 'I'd like that in writing, please, Dr Lindholm.'

'Come on, Miklós, our relationship—'

'I don't care about our relationship,' said my father. 'I want your decision in writing, please. Three copies. I want to send your letter to a superior authority.'

Lindholm got to his feet. He lost his cool. 'Go to hell!' he yelled.

'I'm not going to hell; I'm going to the Hungarian embassy. You are restricting my rights. You are obliged to permit family visits. I'd like your opinion in writing.'

No one had ever spoken like this to Lindholm. He was stunned. He stared at my father. 'Get out!' he said.

Miklós slammed the door and set off down the long corridor. He had surprised himself with his quick thinking. A doctor was restricting his freedom of movement. This was a good argument, effective and true too, more or less. On the other hand, this country had taken him in. And was treating him. Dr Lindholm had every right to claim that restricting his freedom was in his medical interest. In reply, Miklós could point out that the International Red Cross was picking up the bill, not the Swedish state. In other words, he owed his thanks and account-ability ultimately to the Red Cross. If he wanted, say, to spend Christmas in a nightclub in Stockholm, who could stop him?

But what, in fact, was his status here? It was confusing. Was he a patient, a refugee, a dissident or a temporary visitor? His status, yes, his status should be determined somehow. But who should determine it? The Swedish government? The Hungarian embassy? The hospital? Dr Lindholm?

Behind him, in the distance, a door opened and the doctor dashed out. 'Miklós! Come back. We talk it over,' Lindholm shouted down the corridor.

But my father had no intention of arguing his point.

> My darling, my one and only Lili,
> I'm furious and depressed. But I won't give up. I'll think of something.

~

In the afternoons the canteen practically yawned with boredom. It was the only communal area in Berga. The girls didn't have much choice: they could stretch out on their beds in the barracks, go for walks in the biting wind or sit around in this hall crammed with tables and wait for supper.

That afternoon, Lili decided she would have a go at August Bebel's *Woman and Socialism*. Miklós had written to her about it a few times and it was now two months since he had sent her the paperback. Lili had stored it in different places to keep it out of sight. The cover wasn't very inviting: a woman with dilated pupils and bulging eyes, as if she were suffering from goitre, stared out at the reader, her long hair ruffled by the wind.

Lili read for ten minutes, and became more and more angry. By the fourth page, she was incensed. 'This is unreadable!' she said, banging the book shut and hurling it into the furthest corner of the hall.

Sára was knitting a pullover out of Miklós's ugly mud-grey wool, which she had brought with her from Eksjö. 'What's wrong with it?'

'Even the title irritates me. How can a book have a title like that? *Woman and Socialism*. Inside it's even worse.'

Sára put down her knitting and walked over to pick up the book. She dusted it off, returned to the table and handed it to Lili. 'It's a bit dry, I agree. But if you keep going—'

'No chance of that. I'm sick of it! I'd rather read nothing. Sick of it, you hear?'

'It could teach you a thing or two. How Miklós thinks, for example, if nothing else.'

Lili shoved the book away from her as if it were contagious.
'I know how he thinks. This book is unreadable.'

Sára gave up and went back to her knitting.

> Darling Miklós,
>   I'll be sending the Bebel book back shortly.
> Unfortunately the circumstances here — and my
> nerves — aren't conducive to my having the patience
> for a book like that.

Grey light filtered through the big, dusty windows of the canteen. Judit Gold peeped through to see whether Lili and Sára were in there together. Even like this, when they were having an argument, they clearly belonged together. Judit felt superfluous beside them, but her loneliness had never tugged at her heart as keenly as it did now. Would it always be like this? Would she never have anyone for herself? There'd be no men. Fair enough, she'd given up on them, but would she never have a girlfriend, a true, lifelong girlfriend? Would she always have to accommodate herself to other people? Humiliate herself for a caress? Be grateful for a kind word, a piece of advice, a hug? Who was this Lili Reich anyway?

Judit turned away from the window and hurried towards the barracks. Their dormitory was furnished with twelve iron beds. There were metal lockers in an anteroom. Judit walked over and unlocked one. She took out the yellow suitcase with its brass buckle that her cousin from Boston — her only surviving relative—had sent her in August, stuffed with tins of fish. All the sprats, mackerel and herrings had already been eaten or shared with the other girls, but now and then Judit took out the suitcase and ran her hands over it, imagining that one day she would carry it triumphantly down the main street of Debrecen. But perhaps she wouldn't return to Debrecen. Who of her friends and relatives there had survived? She might settle here in Sweden. She would find work, a husband, a home. Yes, a husband! Who knew? Fate is sometimes kind to the determined.

Judit was alone in the barracks. She took a purse out of one of the side pockets of the yellow suitcase where she had hidden it. And now she took the remnant out and clasped it in her hand. Why she had hidden it? Or kept it at all for that matter? It could have been discovered at any time. But she wasn't really worried about that. Who would dare search her suitcase? Unless! Unless those two unpleasant-looking guys from Eksjö were bent on getting to the bottom of the mystery. Better to get rid of it.

The fabric almost burned her palm—this expensive cloth she'd taken such delight in cutting up into strips. She had good reason for doing so. No one on earth could condemn her for that. No one!

Judit ran to the bathroom and locked the door. She took a last sniff of the material and threw it in the toilet, sighing as she pulled the chain. The rushing water hissed and frothed.

Fourteen

DR LINDHOLM had a few sleepless nights before he made
up his mind to phone Lili. He shared his anxieties with Márta.
Miklós's wandering off into the forest had disturbed her. She,
too, felt that everything had got confused and a talk to clarify
things wouldn't do any harm. Dr Lindholm asked Márta to be
present as an impartial observer when he called Lili and to warn
him, with a sign, if he went too far.

After the formalities, he began to make a little speech.
'Miklós's walk in the forest was part about wanting to escape,
and part ... '

Lili pressed the receiver to her ear in the caretaker's office at

Berga. She had hoped it was Miklós calling her and had sprinted for the phone. She waited for her heartbeat to slow after hearing Lindholm's voice. She wished he would get to the point.

'Part?'

'Part about facing facts. For five months have I now am treating him, dear Lili. Never, not once, has he faced up to how sick he really is. I mean it. I am going to say something cruel, Lili. Are you ready for it?'

'I'm ready for anything—and nothing, doctor. But, anyway, go ahead.'

Dr Lindholm was sitting in his comfortable armchair. He took a deep breath. 'Miklós must look death in the eyes. Four times we have to drain his lungs. We can treat his illness but we cannot cure it. Out of misconceived heroism he has ignored the diagnosis. As we doctors say, he is denying it. Are you there, Lili?'

'Yes, I am.'

'Now, when he went into the forest, is the first time for five months that he allowed reality to climb up the ivory tower he builds around himself. We have come to a turning place, Lili. Are you still there?'

'Yes, I am.'

'Unpredictable traumatic effects are normal. Can you help me in this, dear Lili? The answer is not to let Miklós cook his absurd pies in the sky. Are you still there, Lili?'

'Yes, I am.'

'This marriage that he is planning with you is not just absurd and sheer madness. At this stage it could even be damaging.

Miklós is no longer able to tell difference between reality and his imaginary world. You realise how symbolic this rambling was?'

'Symbolic? In what way?'

'A signal of alarm. A warning for me, his doctor, and for you who love him.'

'What do you expect from me?'

'You must end this foolishness. With sincerity. With love. With feeling.'

Lili was leaning against the wall in the caretaker's office, cradling the receiver. Now she pushed herself away from the wall. 'Look, doctor, I respect your exceptional expertise, your rich experience. The sensational achievements of medical research. The pills you prescribe, your X-rays, your cough mixtures, your syringes … I respect everything. But I implore you to leave us in peace. Leave us to dream. And not worry about science. I beg you on my knees. I pray and beseech you, doctor, let us get better! Are you still there?'

Lindholm had beckoned Márta to come over to him so she could hear Lili's passionate plea too. All he could manage now was a sorrowful 'Yes, I am'.

~

Two days before Christmas 1945, Miklós made a desperate decision. He persuaded Harry to go to Berga with him without permission or money.

He had weighed up his options. He would not seek official

approval—that would probably mean labyrinthine battles in an unfamiliar legal system. He knew he should stick to the straight and narrow, but his instincts were telling him otherwise.

To get to Berga, they would have to change trains three times. Three trains, three ticket collectors. Both Miklós and Harry were good at talking their way out of things. They were skinny, badly dressed, unwell. No official could help taking pity on them. They would ride their luck.

On Monday afternoon they walked to Avesta station and boarded a train.

> Dear Lili,
>   What do you think of this? We could place an announcement in the next issue of *Via Svecia* saying, 'We're engaged to be married'. Just that and our names.

> Dear Miklós,
>   Do write and tell Mama too. How will you get the money? Have you written to your acquaintance the bishop yet?

They were disqualified at the first hurdle. The ticket collector looked at them in surprise and asked them twice for their tickets.

Miklós smiled kindly at him. 'We don't have any. We don't have enough money. We're Hungarian patients from the Avesta rehabilitation centre.'

The ticket collector wasn't the slightest bit impressed. He put them off the train at the next station and reported them to the stationmaster.

They had travelled exactly seventeen kilometres. Someone arranged for a bus to transport the two fugitives back to Avesta. On this bus there would be no need for tickets.

In the meantime, a committee was convened to discuss the punishment for my father's wayward behaviour.

> My darling, one and only Lili,
>   Half an hour ago we were transported back here into the midst of a whopping hoo-ha. I can't describe the fuss they made.

~

Dr Lindholm X-rayed Miklós once again. The next day he sent for him to give him his assessment. Miklós sat down and, shutting his eyes, leaned back, balancing on the back two legs of his chair. Now all he had to do was concentrate, keep his balance, and he would find his centre of gravity. If he could keep the front two legs in the air for five seconds then he would be cured. Totally.

Dr Lindholm wanted to talk about his escape attempt. He was gentle today, understanding. 'You bungle that, Miklós. The director and governor of the centre are furious.'

Miklós got himself higher and further back on the chair. 'What can they do?'

'Transfer you.'

'Where?'

'To Högbo, probably. Is a village in the north. My medical opinion counts for nothing.'

'Why? Because I tried to go and see my cousin?'

'For breaking rules. Absence without leave. Don't forget, Miklós, you went missing twice recently. But please know I have nothing against you. Frankly, I understand you. You are thinking what difference it makes anyway?'

Miklós was nearing the tipping point. Was he going to topple over or not? That was the real question. 'What did you see on my lungs yesterday?' he asked.

'I wish I could give you good news but I can't. This X-ray confirms that—'

Crash. In anger Miklós let the front legs of the chair hit the floor. He looked up at the doctor. 'I'm going to get better!'

Lindholm winced at the thud. He avoided my father's gaze.

Lindholm got up and held out his hand. 'You are an odd chap, Miklós. Naïve and compulsive at the same time. Stubborn and a likeable fool. I am fond of you. Is pity we have to part.'

~

My father wasn't the least put out by his expulsion from Avesta, but was rattled to discover, when he looked up Högbo on the map, that it was forty-five kilometres further away from Berga. He walked over to the nurses' room. 'Could I borrow your suitcase again, please?'

Márta went up to my father without a word, stood on tiptoe and kissed his cheek.

'Don't forget to take your pills every morning,' she warned him. 'And give up smoking. Promise me. Let's shake on it.'

They shook hands.

In the afternoon, Miklós started packing. He decided to throw out everything that wasn't necessary, so he could cram his entire life into the battered suitcase. His clothes wouldn't take up much room, but he had a lot of books, notes and newspapers. And then there were all the letters, still in their envelopes, in the huge cardboard box.

Being kicked out of the barracks had created a symbolic opportunity. Now, at last, Miklós could jettison everything he had wanted to get rid of for ages. He took from the cardboard box a thick sheaf of letters tied up with silk ribbon. These were from Lili. He gathered up every other letter from the last five months—from Klára Köves, from a naïve sixteen-year-old girl from the north-east of Hungary, the floods of complaints from two divorced Transylvanian women—and set out with them to the shower room. The fact is, even after he came back from Eksjö in early December, after his three days with Lili, he was still writing to eight girls. He told them all that he was madly in love and soon to be married. Two wrote back to congratulate him.

Miklós took this distinguished bundle of letters out to the shower room and set fire to them. He watched all those words burn, and noted with satisfaction that he was also destroying the smooth-talking charmer who had written so many letters.

That was when he heard the sound of a violin. He waited until everything had turned to ashes and then walked back to the barracks. Harry was standing on a table in the centre of the dormitory playing the 'Internationale'. The men appeared from everywhere, from under beds, from behind cupboards, from behind the door. Ten of them lined up as if they were on a stage.

> Arise, you prisoners of starvation!
> Arise, you wretched of the earth!
> For justice thunders condemnation:
> A better world's in birth!

All my father's friends were singing: Laci, Jóska, Adi, Farkas, Jakobovits and Litzman. Harry's face was the picture of innocence as he played his violin.

> I'm being transferred to Högbo because I'm an
> undisciplined, subversive, disobedient trouble-maker.
> Ten of my friends announced right away that they
> wouldn't stay here for a moment without me. So Laci,
> Harry, Jakobovits and others are coming too.

The men marched out, taking Miklós with them. They paraded through the main building singing. Harry was in the lead with his violin, and the team followed him.

It is the final conflict
Let each stand in his place
The International Union
Shall be the human race.

Dozens of doctors, nurses and office workers poured out into the corridor. Only now were the men aware of the considerable army of people who were looking after them. There were a number of faces that Miklós didn't know. Most of them had never before heard this rousing, powerful song, especially not in Hungarian. But as the ten spirited young men marched and sang, arm in arm, it was victory itself.

My dear Miklós,
  I'm devastated that our wanting to see each other again could be the cause of so much fuss.

Darling Lili,
  Every minute we've spent together was a life for me. I love you so very much! You know, if I think that we've still got months and months to wait before we can be together forever, it puts me in the worst mood.

My one and only Miklós,
  I'll try to get permission here in Berga to come and visit you.

~

The director of the Berga rehabilitation centre offered Lili a seat in her austerely furnished office. She was a thin, severe woman in glasses. Lili wondered if she'd ever smiled in her life. A cardboard box sat on her desk.

'Good to see you, Lili. I've just been speaking to Mr Björkman,' she said, indicating the telephone. 'He asked me to call him as soon as the parcel arrived.' She pushed the box across to Lili. 'It's yours. Go ahead and open it.'

Lili undid the string and tore the box open. She laid the contents out on the table. Two bars of chocolate, a few apples and pears, a pair of nylon stockings and a Bible.

The woman leaned back in her chair with satisfaction. 'Mr Björkman asked me to find a family for you here in Berga.'

Lili leafed through the Bible and saw to her disappointment that it was in Swedish—she wouldn't be able to read a word.

'I see you're wearing the present the Björkmans gave you.'

Lili put her hand on the silver cross. 'Yes.'

'Mr Björkman asked me to give you their love and tell you they remember you in their prayers. They are happy that you've been able to contact your mother. How would you feel if I were to let you spend the weekend with an excellent Catholic family?'

The right moment had come. Lili had planned not to beat around the bush or complicate things—she'd sweep the woman off her feet in a cavalry charge. 'I'm in love!' she declared.

The director was astonished. 'What has that got to do with it?'

'I need help, please! I've fallen in love with a man who is

about to be transferred from Avesta to Högbo. I'd like to visit him. I must!' At last it was out. She put on her most imploring expression.

The woman removed her glasses and, squinting fiercely, wiped them with a handkerchief. She must have been very short-sighted. 'One of the two men who went missing from Avesta last week?'

That sounded rather hostile.

'Yes, but they had reason—' Lili began.

'I disapprove of such behaviour,' the director said. She put her glasses back on and looked at Lili.

'I love him. And he loves me,' said Lili doggedly. 'We want to get married.'

The woman was taken aback. This new information required thought. 'How did you get acquainted?'

'Through letters! We've been writing to each other since September.'

'Have you ever met?'

'He came to visit me a few weeks ago in Eksjö. We spent three days together. I'm going to be his wife.'

The woman drew the Bible towards her and started to leaf through it. She was playing for time. When she looked up, there was so much sorrow in her expression that Lili almost felt pity for her.

'This must be a joke. After four months of letter-writing you want to tie your life to a stranger? I would expect more sense from you.'

Lili realised with dismay that she wouldn't be able to convince this woman. She made one last attempt. 'Are you married?'

'That's totally irrelevant.' The director shut the Bible, took off her glasses and looked down at her spindly fingers. 'I had a fiancé once. He was a great disappointment. An enlightening experience, but a great disappointment.'

Fifteen

RABBI EMIL Kronheim's home in Stockholm could hardly have been described as comfortable. But its dark, heavy furniture had served the rabbi's great-grandfather, grandfather and his father, too. The fraying and faded brocade curtains that hung from the massive windows might have been more than a hundred years old. The rabbi felt safe here. It never occurred to him to get the place painted or to move elsewhere.

There always seemed to be unwashed dishes piled up in the kitchen. Mrs Kronheim was no longer bothered by the smell of herring that hit visitors like an attack of mustard gas. But the rabbi always took a new, clean plate for his herring, and that was the source of frequent quarrels.

Mrs Kronheim was sitting in the kitchen staring at the dozens of oily plates scattered around the place.

'Listen to this,' the rabbi shouted to her from the dining-room table. '"Lili even wants to renounce her Jewishness. She and the man who has ensnared her with his letters are planning to convert. The man has a serious case of TB. On top of that he claims to know a bishop in Stockholm—which I'm sure is a lie. I beg you, Reb, please do something!'

The rabbi was reading out bits of the letter, while picking up and devouring pieces of herring without so much as a glance at his plate.

'Who wrote that?' Mrs Kronheim called from the kitchen.

The rabbi noticed, to his surprise, that stains from the salty liquid in which the herring was pickled were forming strange shapes on the tablecloth.

'A moon-faced girl with a moustache, by the name of'—he looked at the envelope on which oily traces of herring were already visible—'by the name of Judit Gold.'

Mrs Kronheim knew that sooner or later she would have to wash up and the thought gave her no pleasure. 'Do you know her?'

'Yes. I visited her in Eksjö months ago. We talked about flies.'

'One of your cautionary tales, no doubt.'

The rabbi demolished another herring. He smacked his lips. 'She is well meaning and emotional. Not afraid to cry.'

'Who is?' sighed Mrs Kronheim.

'This girl, Judit Gold. But deep inside, at the bottom of her heart, do you know what she's like?'

His wife got to her feet and began to gather up the plates, putting them disconsolately into a bowl.

'No, you tell me. You're such a clever man.'

'She's sad and disturbed,' he said, holding up the letter. 'That's what's she's like inside. This is her third letter. She keeps telling tales on her friend—and maybe not just to me.'

~

Miklós and his loyal friends were moved to a two-storey boarding house in Högbo, a couple of hundred kilometres north of Stockholm. They were greeted by Erik, a hefty man in a suit, who introduced himself as the superintendent and read out the house rules. Apart from being strict about meal times, he didn't really require anything of them. Once a week they would have to go to Sandviken for a check-up. My father had the distinct feeling that the whole thing was a waste of time.

He was even more dejected when they went upstairs to their rooms. Twenty men were housed in three dormitories, which meant that seven beds were crammed into rooms more suitable for a family weekend than a long-term stay. The cupboards had been moved out into the hallway. Erik watched from the doorway as they glumly selected their beds and sat with their suitcases on their laps. None of them was in a hurry to unpack. Erik warned them that smoking in the rooms was forbidden and then disappeared.

> Seven of us live in a cubbyhole: Laci, Harry, Jóska, Litzman, Jakobovits, Farkas and me. So far we don't have a cupboard or a table. Luckily there's central heating. As for the beds! Straw mattresses and the kind of pillow I had in prison.

Miklós picked the bed under the window for himself. He tried not to let the pervasive gloom get a grip. He whistled as he unpacked the photo of Lili and himself from Eksjö. He put it on the sill, propping it up against the windowpane. When he woke up the next morning the first thing he'd see would be Lili's smile.

~

That afternoon Harry and Miklós took a bus into town to visit the jeweller. Harry had brought his violin with him in its case. Erik had warned them that the jeweller was a quibbling old man. Above the door of the shop hung a bronze bell that rang whenever someone entered.

The jeweller, contrary to expectations, was a kindly grey-haired gentleman who wore a purple bowtie.

My father had prepared his strategy. 'I would like to buy two gold wedding rings.'

The jeweller smiled. 'Do you know the sizes?'

Miklós fished a metal ring out of his pocket. He had taken it from a curtain rail in Eksjö. It fitted Lili's finger perfectly.

'This is my fiancée's size. The other one's for me.'

The old man took the ring, estimated its size, and pulled out a drawer in the cupboard behind him. He rummaged around a little.

'Here you are!' he said, holding up a gold ring. He took a gauge from under the counter, compared the two rings to his satisfaction, and slipped the gold ring into his pocket.

'Can I have your finger?' he asked.

He grasped my father's ring finger, pondered a moment, opened a different drawer and chose another ring. 'Try this one on,' he said holding it out to him.

Miklós slipped it on. It was an exact fit.

> I don't like gold; it always makes me think of all the alien, vulgar and wicked emotions associated with it. But I like these two rings; after all they connect your blood with mine.

Miklós and Harry exchanged glances. They'd arrived at the critical moment.

'How much do I owe you?' My father asked.

The old man deliberated. As if he too were brooding over the wicked emotions associated with such a trifle. 'Two hundred and forty kronor, the pair,' he announced.

Miklós didn't flinch. 'I'm living in a boarding house in Högbo—it's a rehabilitation centre.'

The old man straightened his bowtie. 'I've heard something about it.'

'I'd like to take you into my confidence. You see, I've been given an important job there.'

'Oh, a job. Excellent!' The jeweller gave him a friendly smile.

'Yes, and I'll get paid for it. Monthly. I reckon I can save 240 kronor in four months.'

Miklós wasn't making this up. That morning, after the small Hungarian colony, their suitcases on their laps, assessed their wretched situation, the men appointed my father their representative. He promised to stand up for them. And all of them, including the Poles and the Greeks, agreed to set aside a small part of their pocket money each month to pay Miklós for his efforts.

The old man seemed impressed. But he didn't want to be cheated. 'First of all, I congratulate you, young man. This could be the start of a fine career. But, for my part, I made a solemn vow to my mother. I was young at the time and perhaps it was a little rash of me. You know, our family has been in this business for two hundred years. I promised my mother that I would never on any account give credit to anyone. It might seem hard-hearted, but you must agree that a vow made to a mother is binding.'

Miklós, who had planned a two-pronged attack from the outset, nodded earnestly. 'I'm a Hungarian. I'd like you to look me in the eye. You don't think I'm a swindler, do you?'

The jeweller took a step back. 'Certainly not. I can smell swindlers a mile off. I can safely say that you are not the swindling type.'

The moment had come. Miklós gave Harry a kick. Harry sighed, laid his violin case on the counter and opened it. He picked up the violin tenderly and held it out to the old man.

'Well, I was pretty sure you wouldn't give credit to a stranger,' Miklós said, speaking with slow eloquence for heightened effect. 'What I had in mind was to leave this violin here as a pledge until I had saved enough money. It is worth at least four hundred kronor. I hope you'll accept it as security.'

The old man took out a magnifying glass and inspected the violin. It had been given to Harry by the Swedish Philharmonic Orchestra last summer, after a newspaper reported that a young violinist, a concentration camp survivor, was convalescing on the island of Gotland. It was worth a lot more than four hundred kronor. Even the old man's mother would have approved of this.

~

Rabbi Emil Kronheim stumbled off the bus. His legs were stiff from the long journey; it was beastly cold and now it had started to snow again. The rabbi asked where he could find the women's rehab hospital, drew his coat around him and set out.

~

Within a few days Miklós had the opportunity to prove how qualified he was for his elected post.

They were all sitting in the shabby dining room. The ten Hungarians, the Greeks, the Poles and the Romanians. The only sound was the angry beating of spoons as they struck the table in perfect time until Erik, the hefty superintendent, bustled in.

'What's the trouble, gentlemen?' he asked, afraid he wouldn't be heard above the din. Everybody stopped clanging. My father picked up a fork and rose to his feet.

> Just imagine, darling Lili, how grand I've become!
> I've been elected representative of our group. It's not
> much work, but I get paid 75 kronor a month.

Miklós pierced a piece of potato on the prong of his fork and held it up. 'This potato is rotten.'

Erik looked around in embarrassment. Then, since everyone was staring at him and he wanted to live up to his role as superintendent, he sauntered over to my father and put his nose to the potato. 'It smells of fish. What's the problem?' he said, trying not to make a face.

Miklós held the potato aloft as if it were an item of evidence.

'It's rotten. We had our suspicions about the potatoes yesterday, but today they are definitely off.'

A Greek kid, who kept his knitted hat on, even at night, stood up. 'I'll write to the International Red Cross!' he shouted in Greek.

'Pipe down, Theo,' Miklós admonished him. 'I'll deal with this.' He looked at Erik and politely pointed to a chair beside him. 'Sit with us.'

Erik hesitated.

'I'd like you to taste it,' said Miklós, drawing the chair back for him.

Erik sat down tentatively on the edge of the chair. Harry was already bringing him a plate and a knife and fork. My father eased the potato from his fork into the middle of the empty plate.

'Bon appétit,' Miklós said.

Erik looked around in dismay. There was no mercy. He bit into the potato. Miklós sat down beside him, studying him as he chewed and swallowed.

The superintendent tried to make a joke of it. 'It tastes a bit like shark. But I like shark. It's really quite nice.'

'Is that so? Well, if it's quite nice, have some more,' said Miklós with a deadpan expression as he stabbed another potato and put it on Erik's plate.

Erik knew he had to tackle this potato too. It was more difficult to get down, but somehow he managed it.

'Believe me, there's nothing wrong with it. Nothing on earth.'

'Nothing? Well, go on, have some more.'

Miklós sped up. He kept stabbing potatoes and piling them onto Erik's plate. The men were on their feet by this time, crowding around him.

My darling one and only Lili, just imagine, the superintendent turned pale, but he led from the front and right to the end he heroically maintained they were edible.

Erik reckoned his best bet would be to get through this circus as quickly as possible. So he wolfed the potatoes down. 'Quite edible. Not bad at all. Good, in fact.'

But now he was feeling sick. Drinking between every mouthful, he bravely finished off the mound of potatoes. Then he lurched to his feet, clutching the edge of the table to stop himself falling.

Miklós grabbed his shoulders and tried to support him. 'As you very well know, every last potato peel is paid for by the United Nations. I would be obliged if you did not treat us inmates as beggars, expecting us to show our gratitude for every last boiled potato.'

The men started clapping. This is what they were expecting of my father, this tone. This was what he was being paid for.

Erik belched, clutching his stomach. 'You misunderstand the situation,' he spluttered, and then collapsed with stomach pains so severe he had to dig his nails into the floor to stop himself crying out.

Sixteen

ONE HUNDRED and sixty girls ate lunch together in the Berga canteen, where all the tables had been pushed together to form three long rows. Two kitchen maids served the food, along with three patients elected each week to help. It took an hour and a half to serve everyone.

Emil Kronheim was escorted into the canteen by the unsmiling woman in charge—the director. The rabbi had grown accustomed to the bleak, military atmosphere of these places, but they still disheartened him. He had requested a room adjacent to the canteen be made available for him.

Judit Gold was sitting with Lili and Sára a long way from the door, but it was as if she sensed a change in the atmosphere. She couldn't say why she did it, but she glanced at the door just as it opened—and there was the rabbi. Judit turned pale and started to sweat. She willed herself to focus on her spoon as it dipped into the red soup.

The director came over and stopped right beside them. Judit almost buried her head in her soup bowl.

'You've got a visitor,' she whispered in a confidential tone.

Judit looked up. She found it strange that no one could hear her heart beating.

'Me?' asked Lili, getting to her feet.

'Rabbi Kronheim from Stockholm. He'd like to speak to you.'

'A rabbi? From Stockholm? Now?'

'He's in a hurry. He's got to catch the two o'clock train.'

Lili looked over the heads to the doorway where Emil Kronheim was standing. He gave her a friendly nod.

There was a small room next to the canteen, linked to it by a serving window. If Judit sat up straight, she could see into this room, and she couldn't resist peeking from time to time. She saw the two of them introduce themselves and sit at a table. Judit was trembling. She put her spoon down. She was sure the rabbi wouldn't betray her, but her remorse gnawed at her.

The rabbi had put his pocket watch on the table in the small room. He was relying on its quiet tick to create the right atmosphere. They had been listening to it for a while now—Lili had no intention of breaking the silence.

When Rabbi Kronheim felt that the tick-tock effect had been achieved, he leaned forward and looked into Lili's eyes. 'You have lost God.'

The pocket watch ticked away. Lili didn't ask how this stranger had the ability to see into her mind, but his powers of intuition didn't surprise her. 'No, God has lost me.'

'It's beneath you to split hairs on such a question.'

Lili was fiddling with the crocheted tablecloth. 'But what makes you think that about me?'

'It's not important at the moment. I just know.' The rabbi shifted his weight, making the chair creak. 'Have you got a cross, too?'

Lili blushed. How did he know? She felt in her pocket for the envelope where she kept the cross. Since she had come to Berga she had worn it only once, when she went to the director to beg for the visit. It hadn't helped. 'Yes. Yes, I do. It was a gift. Do you object?'

'Well, I'm not exactly thrilled,' he said sadly.

The pocket watch continued to tick.

'Look here, Lili, we are all filled with doubts. Big ones and lesser ones. But that doesn't mean we have to turn our backs.'

Lili thumped the table. The watch bounced like a rubber ball. 'Were you there? Did you come with us?' Lili was whispering, but her fist was clenched and her body was rigid. 'Were you there with us in the cattle wagon?'

The rabbi pointed to the others in the canteen beyond the window. 'I won't insult you by saying it was a test. I wouldn't dare tell you that, after all you've been through. God has lost you—all right. Or rather, it's not all right—I too have an issue with him about that. I'm angry. I don't forgive, either. How could he have done this to us? To you! To them!'

He put his watch away. It had served its purpose. He got to his feet and knocked his chair over. Taking no notice, he started pacing. It was four steps from wall to wall. He strode up and down, passionately waving his arms around.

'No, there can be no forgiveness for that. I, Rabbi Emil Kronheim, am telling you this. But ... but! Millions of your brethren perished. Millions were murdered, like animals in a slaughterhouse. No, even animals are treated better than our fellow Jews were. But, for crying out loud, those millions aren't even cold in their graves yet! We haven't even finished the prayers for them. And you would leave us already? You would turn your back? Don't be fair to God; he doesn't deserve it. Be fair to the millions. You have no right to abandon them.'

From the canteen, Judit Gold could see Kronheim storming around the room and shouting. She felt lucky to be where she was. Here, she had only to put up with the hum of the dining room, the clatter of spoons, the quiet chatter of the girls. She had, however, lost her appetite. She was nauseated even by the thought of the risotto growing cold in her bowl.

~

Darling Miklós,

Today a rabbi came from Stockholm and gave me
a little moral sermon about our conversion. How on
earth did he hear about that? Could your bishop have
told him?

This part of the letter prodded my father into urgent action.
He decided to take a short cut with regard to the complicated
matter of their conversion. He looked up the phone number of
the nearest parish. The less significant the parish, he reckoned,
the less fuss there would be. A country priest would surely be
easier to convince than a bishop from the capital.

He discussed everything on the telephone and a few
days later caught a bus from Högbo to the nearby village of
Gävle.

In Gävle he found the friendly, simple wooden church that
he was secretly hoping for. The light flooded in through the
windows above the gallery. The priest was over eighty and his
head shook constantly. Miklós had gone to the public library
in Högbo the day before and buried himself in canon law in
preparation for the meeting. It was well worth the effort. When
he brought up the term *Congregationes religiosae* and explained
how he and Lili were Jews who wanted to be married in his
church, the old man's eyes shone with tears.

'How do you know about things like that?'

Miklós didn't respond; he went on in a rather self-important
way. 'The main thing is that, instead of taking a solemn vow, my

fiancée and I would only take a simple vow to bind us to the Catholic faith.'

The priest's hands were shaking too. He took out a handkerchief and wiped his eyes. 'I'm very touched by your fervour.'

Miklós was in full swing, and he began to quote, line by line, the relevant passages from the ecclesiastical literature. 'Do correct me if I'm wrong, Father, but as I understand it the simple vow is one-sided. It binds the party that takes the vow—that is, me and my fiancée—to the Church, but it doesn't bind the Church to us. On the other hand the solemn vow would be mutual, meaning that it couldn't be broken by either party.'

'How do you know all this?'

'We are serious about conversion, Father.'

The old man gathered his strength, got to his feet and began striding towards the sacristy. Miklós could hardly keep up with him. The priest took out an enormous leather-bound book and dipped his pen in the ink. Miklós was fascinated that the ink was green.

'You've convinced me. I have no doubts regarding the seriousness of your intentions. I'd like to write down your particulars. You should let me know when your fiancée can travel here from Berga. Once we have the date I will arrange for your baptism right away. I'll say one thing, Miklós, in all my time as a priest I've never come across such touching enthusiasm.'

~

Miklós and Lili now wrote to each other even more often. Sometimes they sent two letters in one day. On New Year's Eve, Miklós went up to his room. He didn't want to get drunk with the men in the boarding-house dining room downstairs. He lay on his bed, put Lili's photo on his chest and swore he would stay alive. He kept repeating this until he fell asleep. Towards dawn Harry and the others staggered in. They found my father lying on his back fully dressed, with tears trickling down his cheeks in his sleep and Lili's photo peeping out from under his hand.

> Darling Lili,
>   Damn the *Via Svecia*! I ordered the notice,
> sending in the exact wording, and they go and publish
> it with a shocking mistake. They mixed up the names!
> According to the notice, you asked for my hand! I
> hardly feel like sending it to you.

~

New Year's Eve in Berga began with Lili playing the piano and Sára singing. They had practised some songs from operettas — 'Péter Hajmási' from *The Csárdás Queen* was such a success they had to perform three encores. The rest of the evening was less cheerful. The three-piece band played, a lot of girls danced, and a lot cried, too. They had each been given a litre of red wine with supper.

> I thought of you today at lunchtime because we had
> tomato sauce, and I know you love that! Oh, how I
> love you, my little sweetie-pie!

~

On New Year's Day the men made resolutions. Ever since he'd
been allowed to get out of bed, in July, Pál Jakobovits had been
secreting a slice of bread into his pocket at every meal. He was
aware of the stupidity of this; after all, there would always be
bread here. But force of habit was stronger. On 1 January 1946,
he resolved not to stuff his pocket with bread from that day on.
Harry swore not to chat girls up unless he felt there was love
involved. Litzman decided to emigrate to Israel. Miklós resolved
to start learning Russian as soon as he got back to Hungary.

> When we daydream together, we think of everything,
> not only a self-serving love. We imagine a future
> together, working, following our vocations, in the
> service of mankind and society.

On the morning of New Year's Day in Berga the Hungarian
girls sang the national anthem.

> My one and only darling Miklós,
> When are you going to the dentist in Stockholm?

~

A week later Miklós caught the bus to Sandviken, about half an hour away. He sat alone. It was one of the coldest winters for years—this day it was minus twenty-one degrees Centigrade. Thick ice coated the windows. The bus looked as if it had been wrapped in tin foil. It jolted along in its silver splendour.

> At home I only want to work for a left-wing newspaper and, if I can't find anything, I'll look around for some other occupation. I'm sick of the bourgeoisie.

On the same morning, in Berga, Lili refused to get out of bed. At about midday Sára and Judit pulled her up by force. They even dressed her, like a doll. They had found a sled somewhere, and they put Lili on it and took turns pulling her up and down the main pathway.

> My darling Miklós,
>   I've never ever felt as homesick as I do now. I'd give ten years of my life to be able to fly home.

My father sat on the bus like a forgotten chocolate in a box wrapped in silver paper. He could forget the outside world. The engine hummed. It was warm inside, the lighting was magical, and the springs rocked him. He put his hand in his pocket and felt something slim and pointed.

> I reached into my pocket and found a Mitzi Six carmine lipstick. I bought it the other day and forgot

to send it to you. I'll be able to give it to you in
person soon. First of all we'll check out whether it's
kiss-proof. All right?

Lili was flying along on the sled. This time Sára and Judit
were pulling it together. They were determined to cheer Lili
up, and hoped that whizzing around in this clear, cold weather
would have the desired effect.

Your letter's in front of me and I've read it about
twenty times. Every time, I discover something new in
it, and every moment I am madder and madder with
happiness.
How I love you!!!
Last night I had a dream that I can't get out of my
mind. It was so clear. We had arrived home. Mama
and Papa were at the train station to meet me. You
weren't with me. I was alone.

In her dream Lili arrived at Keleti station in Budapest.
Crowds of people were waiting but there was no pushing or
shoving. People stood stiffly, staring straight ahead. The only
movement in the dream was the train ceremoniously puffing its
way alongside the covered platform. The smoke enveloped the
crowd. Then it cleared, and in the grey light of dawn passengers began to step down from the train, carrying heavy suitcases.
Those who were meeting them, several hundred, maybe several
thousand, were waiting, transfixed.

Lili was wearing a red polka-dot dress and a wide-brimmed hat. She caught sight of her mother and father in the motionless crowd. She started running, but didn't get a step nearer to them. She was trying so hard to run that her mouth became dry and she could barely breathe. But she couldn't bridge the distance between them. It couldn't have been more than ten metres. Lili could see her mother's sad, lustreless eyes. Luckily, her father was laughing. He held his arms out wide to hug his little girl, but Lili couldn't reach him.

~

The X-ray room in Sandviken was very small; there was space only for the apparatus. By this time Miklós considered X-rays his personal enemy. He had pressed his narrow shoulders so many times against the cold pane of glass that he felt acute loathing if he even glanced at an X-ray machine.

He closed his eyes and tried to stifle his feeling of disgust.

It wasn't possible for Miklós to cultivate a close relationship with his new doctor, Irene Hammarström, as he had with Lindholm—though Irene was compassionate, softly spoken and delicately pretty. She always gave my father a searching look, as if she were trying to fathom his secret.

Now, she stood by the window and held the X-ray up to the light. Miklós played his usual game. He put his weight on the two back legs of the chair and pushed off. He didn't look at her; he was steering the chair into an increasingly precarious position.

'I can't believe my eyes,' gasped the doctor.

Miklós was at the point where a fraction of a millimetre mattered. If he miscalculated, he would crash down like a bowling pin.

Irene Hammarström didn't waste time. She walked over to the table and picked out an older X-ray from the file. She went back to the window and compared the two. 'Look, this is June. The patch is the size of a thumbnail,' she said to Miklós, who had eased himself back a smidgeon.

My father's act had reached its climax. The chair was balancing and his feet were dangling in the air.

'This is today. It's hardly visible. Miraculous! What did Dr Lindholm tell you?'

Miklós had reached his zenith. After all his practice he could balance on the chair between heaven and earth like a motionless falcon about to swoop.

'He said I had six months to live.'

'Somewhat brutal, but the truth. I wouldn't have been able to say anything different.'

My father's one-man show was still running. 'What do you mean by that?'

'Now I'm not quite sure, looking at this latest X-ray.'

'What do you mean?'

'Now, I'd probably encourage you. Tell you to keep up the good work. What about your high temperature? Your dawn fever?'

The show was over, but those five seconds would live on, in the land of miracles. Miklós crashed backwards onto the floor.

'Good Lord!' Irene dropped the X-rays and rushed over to him.

My father had hit the back of his head pretty hard, but he was smiling. 'It's nothing, nothing. I made a bet with myself, that's all.'

Seeing Miklós's ghastly metal dentures, the doctor decided to refer her grinning patient to the district centre in the hope that they could sort out this amicable young Hungarian's teeth for a reduced price, or even for no fee.

~

It was a memorable day. When Miklós returned to the boarding house he found the men waiting for him upstairs, standing to attention. He couldn't imagine how they knew he was on the road to recovery. But as their faces were shining with pride and joy, he reckoned it must be the reason for this performance. He sat down on his bed and waited.

Then the men began to hum Beethoven's 'Ode to Joy'.

When the mystery of the ceremony became unbearable, when the humming chorus of the *Ninth Symphony* had reached its hymnal climax, when my father leaned back on his bed and with eyes shut started to soar, Harry brought out the newspaper. Without a word he held it up in front of Miklós.

There was the poem, in black and white. On page three of

Via Svecia. In Swedish. In italics. *'Till en liten svensk gosse'* ('To a Little Swedish Boy'). Above it was the name of the poet: my father.

~

Miklós composed all his poems in his head. Days and weeks later, when he felt the poem was ready, all he had to do was write it out.

He had finished this poem, however, in about ten minutes. He was sitting in a deck chair on the ship, munching biscuits, savouring the taste of raspberry and vanilla. The ship's horn bellowed, and they drew away from the shore. The women on their bicycles were watching; not one of them stirred. There, an arm's length away, was the country that would take him in, for who knew how long. Miklós felt this sweet gift should be reciprocated. He would write a poem for Swedish children. Advice about life, a warning that would draw its power from his infernal experiences.

He turned the crumbly biscuit in his mouth and set out the first two lines in his head. 'You have yet to learn, little brother, of the deep furrows ploughed across the forehead of a continent.' And now he could see the blond six-year-old child to whom his poem was addressed, who stood staring at him, hugging his teddy. The little Swedish boy.

The lines poured out; it was almost more difficult to remember them than to create them. By the time the ship had turned round and reached the open sea, the poem was finished.

You have yet to learn, little brother,
of the deep furrows ploughed across the forehead of a
     continent.
Here, in the north, you saw an aeroplane
dipped in starlight on a moonlit night.

You didn't know what air-raid warnings or bombs were,
or what it is to survive what's on the film—
the troubles of the world weren't washed
by evil waves onto the children, making them suffer.

Here you had points for clothes, meat rations and bread
     tickets;
you could play sometimes, though, little brother!
But your skinny playmates were burnt in the flames,
and death grinned at its meagre bread.

By the time you grow up and become a man,
a kind, smiling blond giant,
all these falling tears will be clouds,
this age will be history, a hazy vision.

If you muse on this bloody age,
remember a pale little boy—
his plaything was a scrap of grenade,
his minders murderous weapons.

If you have a son, little brother, teach him
that the truth is never a gun or revolver;
and it's not the long range of the rocket
that relieves the suffering of the world.

And in the toyshop, little brother, don't buy
soldiers for your son; on the white toy shelf
let there be wooden blocks, so that in his childhood
he'll learn to build and not to kill.

Harry gave Miklós a pat on the shoulder. 'I took your career in hand. I sent your poem to a Swedish newspaper, anticipating your approval. I asked them to translate it, telling them not to commission any old translator with the task because this was the work of a great Hungarian poet. You. That was three months ago. And this morning it appeared in print. I had the translation checked. It's good.'

The others were still standing up straight, humming 'Ode to Joy'. Miklós got to his feet and gave Harry a hug, concentrating on holding back his tears. Crying wouldn't befit a great Hungarian poet.

~

This really was a fateful day—as Miklós was to discover.

It wasn't yet midnight. Someone was hammering on the door, calling my father's name—there was a man on the phone for him. Miklós woke up. For a moment he had no idea where he was. He found his way downstairs to reception in his pyjamas, his heart thumping.

'Did I wake you?' The voice on the line was unfamiliar.

'It doesn't matter.'

'I apologise. I'm Rabbi Kronheim from Stockholm. I want to speak to you on a matter of importance.'

Miklós's feet were cold; he pressed one sole against his calf. 'I'm listening.'

'Not over the phone! What are you thinking?'

'Sorry.'

'Listen, Miklós, I'm catching the train from Stockholm to Sandviken in the morning. I've got two hours before I have to catch the train back. Let's meet halfway.'

'I can meet you in Sandviken if you like.'

'No, no, I insist on halfway. Will Östanbyn be all right?'

Östanbyn was the first stop after Högbo on the bus to Sandviken. Miklós had passed through it many times.

'Where in Östanbyn?'

'Get off the bus and walk towards Sandviken. Take the first right and keep going until you come to a wooden bridge. I'll be waiting for you there. Got it?'

'Okay.' Miklós was in a daze. 'Could you tell me your name again, please?'

'Emil Kronheim. So, 10 a.m. at the wooden bridge. Don't be late.'

The rabbi hung up. It was all so fast that Miklós realised, with the receiver buzzing in his hand, that he had forgotten to ask what the rabbi wanted to discuss.

~

Miklós followed the rabbi's directions and got off the bus in Östanbyn. He took the first right. He must have been walking briskly for about twenty minutes before he saw the wooden bridge. At the far end a man in a black ankle-length coat was resting on a big stone. Miklós was amazed that anyone could sit still in this frozen world. In fact, he looked as if he were enjoying a summer picnic beside a lake.

'What's the news?' the rabbi yelled across the bridge in a cheerful tone.

Miklós stopped. Not only was the news good, it was positively splendid. But who knew what that grotesque figure over there was talking about?

'Rabbi Kronheim?'

'Who else? Who is this Catholic bishop? The one you promised to Lili? If it is the bishop of Stockholm, I know him well. He's a charming man.'

Lili's letter about a rabbi who lectured her on morality flashed into Miklós's mind. Of course, this was Emil Kronheim! Miklós understood everything! The rabbi had come to chastise him. To hell with it! To think he had made a pilgrimage to Östanbyn for that.

'We don't need the bishop any more.'

'I'll wager you've found someone else.'

The wooden bridge was at least thirty metres long. In the valley below, ancient pine trees were standing guard, silence frozen in the light on their snow-covered branches. There wasn't a breath of wind, no birdsong. The sublime beauty of the countryside was disturbed only by their shouting.

'Well guessed, Rabbi. An excellent old man in Gävle. He will baptise us.'

On the other side of the bridge, Kronheim ran his fingers through his wiry hair. 'Lili isn't so keen now on that silly idea.'

Miklós decided it was time to look the man in the eye. He walked across the bridge and held out his hand. 'She wrote just the opposite to me.'

'What did she write?'

'That a rabbi from Stockholm had preached her a sermon. Somehow or other he had sniffed out our intentions. Something like that.'

'Your lovely fiancée would never have used such a cynical expression. Sniffed out, indeed! I'm not a bloodhound.'

'Seriously, Rabbi, how did you find out? We haven't spoken to a soul about it.'

Kronheim took my father's arm and walked with him to the middle of the bridge. He leaned against the railing and gazed at the scene below.

'Have you ever seen anything as magnificent? It's looked like this for a hundred years. Even a thousand.'

The valley was eerily impressive. Dense pines as far as the eye could see, sprinkled all over with icing sugar.

Miklós decided it was time to leap the last hurdle. 'Look

here, before the war I'd have considered this a way to escape. But now it's a clear and independent decision.'

Kronheim didn't look at my father. He had surrendered to the wonder of nature. 'This landscape is utterly unspoilt.'

'I'm thinking of the fate of our unborn children,' said my father, determined to continue. 'In any case, I've never been a believer. I'm an atheist, and you can despise me for that. But I'd like you to know that our conversion has nothing to do with cowardice.'

The rabbi appeared not to have heard a word. 'It's been here from time immemorial. This bridge, for instance, was designed for people to admire the view. But they made sure to build it out of wood. Can you see any alien material here? Iron, glass or brass? You can't, can you, son?'

'Is this what you wanted to talk to me about, Reb, the wooden bridge at Östanbyn?'

'Among other things.'

Miklós was fed up with all this riddling talk. Just when he was getting the better of his misgivings, this little wiry-haired man turns up and preaches to him about the pristine country-side. He understood him, of course he understood him. Several thousand years—you bet! But if Lili wanted to convert, he would sweep away every worry or hesitation that lay in her path.

He bowed. 'I'm glad to have met you, Rabbi Kronheim. Our decision is final. No one can dissuade us. Goodbye.'

And he strode off in the direction he had come from. At the end of the bridge he turned round. It was as if Emil Kronheim had been waiting for him to do that. The rabbi pulled a letter out of his coat pocket and waved it.

'I hate myself for this,' he shouted. 'But as the scripture says … or maybe it doesn't. Anyway, the main thing is I want to strike a dirty deal with you, son.'

Miklós stared at him, baffled.

'Come and see what I've got.' The rabbi was still holding the letter in the air.

Miklós reluctantly retraced his steps.

'I've written this request; it's so heartfelt that no eye will remain dry. You sign it and I'll take it to Stockholm today. They'll agree, have no worries about that. On one condition: I'd like to be the one who joins you in marriage at the synagogue in Stockholm. Naturally under a *chuppah*. I'll foot the bill for clothes, the ceremony and a reception for your friends. After that the Red Cross will be obliged to offer you, as newlyweds, a room of your own, say, in Berga.'

My father took the letter. It was written in Swedish. As far as he could make out it was addressed to the Stockholm head-quarters of the Red Cross.

'They don't deal with cases like this.'

'Yes, they do. They'll be proud to. They'll pull out all the stops. Make good use of it. Get the story into the newspapers. After all, two young people under their patronage, struggling to live again after all but dying, have forged a commitment to a new life together. By the way, what does your doctor say?'

'About what?'

'Your TB.'

'So you know about that, too?'

'It's my duty to find out. That's what I'm paid for.'

'I'm getting better. The cavity is calcifying.'

'Thank God!' Kronheim gave my father a hug. 'Do we have a deal?' he whispered.

Miklós softened. He was already composing the letter to Lili in which he would explain that a grown-up person—especially if he's a socialist—doesn't quibble over trifling religious questions.

Seventeen

EVERYTHING HAPPENED quickly. The rabbi, as promised, procured the relevant permits. Within two months Lili and my father found themselves in the synagogue in Stockholm under the *chuppah*. Kronheim paid for the rental of a white taffeta dress for Lili and a dinner jacket for my father, and organised a reception after the wedding. The King of Sweden, Gustav V, sent a congratulatory telegram to the young couple who, having barely survived the concentration camp, were now about to swear their undying love.

In February 1946, before the wedding, my father suffered for weeks in a dentist's chair. Kronheim had insisted he swap his alloy teeth for porcelain.

'It can't be much fun kissing you, son,' he said one day. 'I've been talking to my congregation and they unanimously decided to raise the funds for the dental work. They collected six hundred kronor in three days. I've been in touch with a first-class man for the job. Here's his address.'

~

Emil Kronheim could have rubbed his hands. He really had pulled this whole thing off. But before the wedding, at the beginning of March, a visitor arrived to dampen his happiness.

It began with two long impatient rings of the doorbell. The rabbi was eating herring, as usual, and chuckling to himself as he read an American comic. His wife let the visitor into the flat and was so shocked by the stranger's distracted appearance that she led her into the main room without taking her coat, fur cap and snow-covered galoshes. The rabbi didn't even notice her as he lifted a bit of herring out of the brine.

Mrs Kronheim restrained herself from slapping his hand. 'You've got a visitor,' she hissed.

The rabbi stood up in embarrassment, wiping his hands on his trousers. Mrs Kronheim made a distressed sound. 'Your trousers! Dear God!'

There were snowflakes on the young woman's upper lip. She looked like a female Santa Claus.

'Ah, my conscientious letter writer! Sit down,' Kronheim said, offering her a seat.

Judit sat, not even unbuttoning her coat. Mrs Kronheim left discreetly and went into the kitchen.

'I saw you in Berga, Rabbi. Thank you for not giving me away.'

'How about a little salted herring?' he asked, pushing the plate of fish towards her.

'No, thanks. I don't like it.'

'What is there not to like about salted herring? It's full of vitamins. Full of life. Now why would I have given you away, dear Judit? I'm grateful to you for the last-minute warning.'

The snow on Judit's galoshes was melting.

'No, the last minute is now!'

'Good God, did you come all the way to Stockholm to tell me that?'

Judit grabbed the rabbi's hand. 'We have to save Lili.'

'Save her? From whom? From what?'

'From marriage! I can't believe it. My friend wants to get married.'

Kronheim would have liked to withdraw his hand, but her grip was tight. 'Love is a wonderful thing,' he said. 'Marriage is its seal.'

'But the man who wants to marry her is a scoundrel. A marriage con man.'

'My gosh, that's no joke. What makes you think that, Judit?'

Mrs Kronheim came in with homemade vanilla biscuits and tea.

The rabbi hated anything sweet. 'Help yourself to tea. Relax. I'll stick to herring if you don't mind.'

Judit took no notice of the biscuits or the tea. Nor did she notice that the tile stove was pouring warmth into the room of imposing furniture. She didn't even loosen her scarf. 'Listen to me, Rabbi. You don't know everything, so just listen. Imagine a man who gets hold of the names and addresses of all the Hungarian girls convalescing in rehab hospitals in Sweden.'

'I can imagine him.'

'Now imagine that he sits down and writes a letter to each of them. Do you follow? To every single one of them.'

'I see a determined man before me,' said the rabbi, picking up another piece of herring.

'The letters are identical. The same sickly sweet wording. As if he'd made carbon copies. He then walks to the post office and posts the lot. Can you picture it?'

'Oh, that can't be true. Where did you hear that?'

Judit Gold gave the rabbi a triumphant look. Her moment had come. She took a crumpled letter out of her bag. 'Look at this. I got one too. In September last year. Of course I had no intention of replying. I saw through his tricks. What do you say to that? Lili received an identical letter. I saw it and read it. The only difference was the name. You can check it for yourself.'

Kronheim smoothed out the letter and studied it.

Dear Judit,
      You are probably used to strangers chatting you

up when you speak Hungarian, for no better reason
than they are Hungarian too. We men can be so
bad-mannered. For example, I addressed you by
your first name on the pretext that we grew up in the
same town. I don't know whether you already know
me from Debrecen. Until my homeland ordered
me to 'volunteer' for forced labour, I worked for
the *Independent* newspaper, and my father owned a
bookstore in Gambrinus Court.

'Very odd,' remarked the rabbi, shaking his head.

Judit was on the verge of tears. 'And Lili wants to tie the boat
of her life to this crook.'

Kronheim put another herring dreamily into his mouth.
'The boat of her life. How lyrical. Tie the boat of her life to him.'

~

More than fifty years later, when I questioned Lili, my mother,
about the moment she decided to reply to Miklós's letter, she
searched for a long time among her buried memories.

'I don't remember exactly. You know, in September, after
the ambulance took me from Smålandsstenar to Eksjö, during
my second week of being confined to bed, Sára and Judit turned
up in the ward. They brought some of my personal things from
Smålandsstenar—including your father's letter. Judit sat on my
bed and tried to persuade me to write back, prattling on about
how much that poor ill boy from Debrecen must be hoping for

a reply. Then the girls left and I was stuck in bed. I wasn't even allowed to go out to the bathroom. I lay there bored, with your father's letter beside me. Two or three days later I asked the nurses for pencil and paper.'

~

Lili and Miklós were assigned to the second transport of Hungarian returnees, in June 1946. They flew from Stockholm to Prague and caught a train to Budapest the same day.

They held hands in the crowded compartment. After they crossed the border into Hungary my father got up, with an apologetic smile, and made his way to the tiny, filthy toilet and locked the door. As usual his thermometer was in his pocket in its elegant metal case. The train rattled along on the newly repaired track. Miklós stuck the thermometer in his mouth, shut his eyes and clung to the doorhandle. He tried to count to 130 in time to the clattering of the wheels. When he got to ninety-seven he glanced up, and in the cracked mirror above the basin he saw a thin, unshaven man in glasses and an oversized jacket with a thermometer pressed between his lips. He peered closely at the mirror image. Was this what he'd see for the rest of his life? This cowardly looking fellow hooked on his thermometer?

He came to a decision. Without looking at the level of the quicksilver, he yanked the thermometer out of his mouth and chucked it down the toilet. He threw the metal case in as well. Then, determined and angry, he flushed twice.

By nine o'clock on that June evening in 1946 a huge crowd was gathered at Keleti station, even though this was a special train and its arrival hadn't been announced on the radio. But the word had got round. Lili's mother, for instance, heard about the train on the number six tram. A woman in a headscarf had yelled the news down the tramcar during the afternoon rush hour. She also had a daughter coming home after nineteen months away.

Lili was wearing a red polka-dotted dress; during the spring she had begun to put on weight and was now seventy kilos. Miklós's trousers still hung off him; he left Sweden weighing fifty-three kilos. They travelled in the last carriage.

My father stepped onto the platform first, carrying the two suitcases. Mama rushed over to Lili and they hugged each other without speaking. Then she hugged Miklós, who had no family to meet him.

Lili's mother hoped that her husband would make it back. The truth was, however, that Sándor Reich, suitcase salesman, returning home from Mauthausen concentration camp, found his way into a storeroom filled with food. He ate smoked sausage and bacon and was taken to hospital that same night. Two days later he died from a ruptured bowel.

It was a dusty, humid evening. Lili, her mother and Miklós wandered through the excited crowd. They couldn't stop looking at each other. They were at home together.

For the next two years I was in the making, silent and yearning.

Epilogue

MY PARENTS, Miklós and Lili, wrote to each other for six months, between September 1945 and February 1946, before they were married in Stockholm.

Until my father died in 1998, I had no idea the letters still existed. Then, with hope and uncertainty in her eyes, my mother gave me two neat bundles of envelopes bound in silk ribbon, one cornflower blue, the other scarlet.

I was familiar with the story of how they met. 'Your father swept me off my feet with his letters,' my mother would say, and make that charming wry face of hers. She might mention Sweden, that misty, icy enigmatic world at the edge of the map.

But for fifty years I did not know that their letters still existed. In the midst of political upheaval and the chaos of moving to new apartments, my parents had carted them around without ever talking about them. They were preserved by being invisible. The past was locked up in an elegant box it was forbidden to open.

Now I could no longer ask my father about what happened. My mother answered most of my questions with a shrug. *It was a long time ago. You know how shy your father was. We wanted to forget.*

Why? How could they forget a love so wonderfully uninhibited and so splendidly gauche that it still shines? If there were difficult moments in my parents' marriage—and every marriage has its share of them—why didn't they ever untie the ribbons to remind themselves of how they found each other? Or can we allow ourselves a more sentimental line of questioning? In their fifty-two-year relationship wasn't there a moment when time stood still? When the angels passed through the room? When one of them, out of pure nostalgia, longed to dig out the bundles hidden at the back of the bookcase, the testimony of how they met and fell in love?

Of course, I know the answer: there was no moment like that.

~

In one of his letters my father writes that he is planning a novel. He wanted to describe the collective horror of being transported to a German concentration camp—a book (*The Long Voyage*) Jorge Semprún later wrote instead of him.

Why didn't he ever get down to writing it?

I can guess the answer. My father arrived home in June 1946. His younger sister was his only living relative, and his parents' house had been bombed. His past had evaporated. His future, however, was taking shape. He became a journalist and started writing for a left-wing paper. Then, one day early in the 1950s, he found his desk had been moved outside the editorial office.

When exactly did my father lose his faith in communism? I don't know. But by the time of the show trial of László Rajk in 1949 it must have been shattered. And during the revolution in 1956 my parents were concerned primarily with the possibility of emigrating.

I remember my father standing in desperation in our kitchen, which was reeking as usual with the smell of boiling sheets. 'Do you want me to wash dishes for the rest of my life? Is that what you want?' he hissed at my mother.

They stayed.

During the Kádár era, between 1956 and 1988, my father became a respected foreign-affairs journalist. He was founder and deputy editor of *Magyarország*, a quality weekly newspaper. He never wrote the novel about the journey in the railway wagon, and he stopped writing poetry.

This leads me to record the sad fact that in my father's hands neither his own experiences nor those of his companions in distress became a literary work.

I'm convinced that the idea of a new future, the belief that grew into a religion at the beginning, was later cancelled out by his resigned submission to the political circumstances that undermined his aspirations as a writer too. This proves that talent alone is not enough. It doesn't hurt to have luck in life as well.

But my parents took great care of the letters. That's what matters. They kept them safe, until my mother's decision and my father's approving wave from the next world allowed them to reach me.

Reading Group Guide

1. Discuss the author's decision to narrate the novel from Miklós's perspective. Why does the son narrate from his father's perspective? At what point do you know who the narrator's mother is? What kind of narrative distance does this create, and how did it affect your reading?

2. The events of the novel are based on a true story. Did you know this before you started reading? If so, how did it affect your reading of the story? Why do you think the author chose to write this as a novel instead of as nonfiction?

3. Did you learn anything new historically from reading this novel? What surprised you?

4. Why did Miklós persist in writing his letters? What did they mean to him?

5. The opening chapter depicts "an army of women" on bicycles delivering freshly baked biscuits for the survivors arriving in Sweden. What other acts of kindness are described in the novel? How do these contribute to the book as a whole?

6. The author, Péter Gárdos, is also a filmmaker. Where could you see evidence of this in the writing?

7. The doctor gives Miklós very specific measures to guide him toward health: weight, temperature, x-ray results. How does this contrast with Miklós's nature as a poet? What does his temperature each morning come to mean to him — that is, why is the novel called *Fever at Dawn*?

8. What are Miklós's politics before and after the war? Does Lili share these views? Do his fellow Hungarians or the Swedes? (Does it matter?)

9. Talk about the idea of hope. What does it do for Miklós and Lili? How does hope help (or harm) us as humans in such extreme situations? Are there any other stories of hope that this story reminded you of?

10. After Lili and Miklós finally meet, the author writes, "But they never spoke about certain important things. Neither then, nor later." Why do you think they both silently, but mutually, agreed to do this? What do you think avoiding these topics meant for them and their relationship?

11. Lili and Miklós each have their own group of friends whom they confide in about the letters. How did these friendships affect their letter writing and relationship? And how were Lili's and Miklós's friends influenced by their love story?

12. Why do you think Judit betrayed Lili to the rabbi? Why didn't she want Lili and Miklós to get together? Were you sympathetic to her at all? How do you think the traumatic events she's suffered affect her choices here? How did their experiences of the war change — or not — all of these characters?

13. What role do you think humor plays in Lili and Miklós's relationship?